Super Edition

THE GIRLS OF CANBY HALL

THE ALMOST SUMMER CARNIVAL

EMILY CHASE

SCHOLASTIC INC.
New York Toronto London Auckland Sydney

No part of this publication may be reproduced in whole or in part, or stored in a retrieval system, or transmitted in any form or by any means, electronic, mechanical, photocopying, recording, or otherwise, without written permission of the publisher. For information regarding permission, write to Scholastic Inc., 730 Broadway, New York, NY 10003.

ISBN 0-590-40745-7

Copyright © 1987 by Diane Hoh. All rights reserved. Published by Scholastic Inc. THE GIRLS OF CANBY HALL is a registered trademark of Scholastic Inc.

12 11 10 9 8 7 6 5 4 3 2 1   7 8 9/8 0 1 2/9

Printed in the U.S.A.   01

First Scholastic printing, July 1987

Super Edition

THE GIRLS
OF CANBY HALL

THE ALMOST
SUMMER CARNIVAL

THE GIRLS
OF CANBY HALL

CHAPTER ONE

"Hand me the glue, please, Andy," October Houston asked one of her roommates. Andrea Cord and Toby were part of a large group sitting on new spring grass in front of Baker House, their dorm building. The group included several boys from nearby Oakley Prep. The boys' school and the girls from Canby Hall were preparing for the Almost Summer Carnival, put on jointly by the two schools. Surrounded by squares of heavy cardboard, pots of red, green, and blue paint, and cans of soda to sustain them, the group was engaged in the business of making signs for carnival booths.

"Andre-ah!" Toby Houston repeated in her slow Texas drawl, shaking her short red hair impatiently, "toss me the glue!"

The slender black girl with thick dark hair grinned. "Need to pull yourself together, Toby?" But she tossed the tube of glue. Even that small gesture demonstrated the natural grace apparent in Andy's every move. Dancing on a stage or walking across campus, her motions were a combination of strength and grace. Both would be required in her goal to become a ballet dancer of international fame, which no one who knew her well doubted she would achieve.

"So what's the verdict?" she asked now, holding up a sign with the words "RING TOSS" splashed across it in bold green letters. Four small bluebirds decorated the edges of the cardboard.

"Oh, Andy," Jane Barrett exclaimed, laughing, "do you *have* to be so artistic all the time? I mean, what's with the little blue birds?"

Jane was the third member of the trio residing in Room 407 of Baker House. Tall and fine-boned, her long blonde hair was caught up in a ponytail fastened with an elegant gold clip. Andy had no doubt the clip was real gold. The Barretts of Boston didn't believe in fake anything. They didn't have to. Every Barrett in Boston could afford the real thing.

"What's wrong with a little artistic license?" Andy asked.

Cary Slade, Jane's boyfriend, grinned. "Yeah, Jane," he agreed, "loosen up! Is there a law in Massachusetts that says we can't have fun with our carnival signs? I'm putting little squiggly green worms on mine." And he proceeded to do just that.

"Yuk!" Jane yanked at Cary's blond hair,

almost as long as hers. Cary sang with a rock band, Ambulance, while he attended Oakley Prep. He seemed to take a certain amount of pride in announcing that to the world through his style of dress, including one gold earring. Although Cary came from Jane's own proper Bostonian background, he preferred to separate himself from that history as much as possible. Jane, on the other hand, clung to it with pride. "Why worms?" she asked in a voice heavy with disgust.

"Simple." Cary held up his sign. "FISH TANK," he read aloud. "They're going to be fishing for prizes in a tank of sand, right? So why not a few adorable little worms to catch their attention?"

"I hate to tell you this, Cary," Jane said, grinning, "but nobody uses worms for bait when they go fishing in a tank of sand."

Cary shrugged good-naturedly. "So? It's a carnival. Things are supposed to be a little bizarre."

"Oh, no, Cary," Andy said solemnly, "this is not a bazaar. It's a carnival. Didn't anyone *tell* you?"

Toby smiled. Being a Texas rancher's daughter, she saw things differently from her roommates. But in spite of their differences, they were good friends. What would Toby have done without Jane and Andy there to teach her things she'd never had a chance to learn, things like how to dance and how to dress and how to talk to boys? Since her own mother's death years before, there really hadn't been anyone she could ask about such things. Her father wouldn't know the answers. Which was, Toby knew, why he'd sent her here, over her vehement objections. The funny thing was, until she'd come to Canby Hall, she'd never even known those questions were inside her. Her father was pretty smart for a man who, unlike the Barretts, had never seen a finger bowl or an artichoke in his whole life.

Toby sat back on her cowboy boots, her green eyes surveying the campus. Ordinarily it was quiet on a Saturday afternoon, when many of the girls walked in to the village for a little shopping. But with the carnival fast approaching, there were clusters of students scattered about the lawns in front of Addison and Charles Houses as well as Baker. Toby could hear them laughing and talking as they worked on their assignments. It was a beautiful New England spring day, fresh-aired and blue-skied, the huge old trees above them just beginning to leaf out. The tulip and daffodil beds, pride and joy of Patrice Allardyce, Canby's cool, elegant headmistress, were in full bloom. After years of wildflowers and cactus, Toby was intrigued with the bright reds and yellows of the beds. She disliked the clusters of black tulips (what was the point, she wondered, of a *black* flower?) but had been told that the flower was Ms. Allardyce's favorite. And somehow that made sense. Like it or not, the tall black flower *was* impressive. So was the headmistress.

"We need to line up volunteers for the dunking booth," Andy announced, retrieving Toby's attention.

"Jane will volunteer," Cary said with a straight face. "We'd all love to see how Jane looks with her preppy clothes and her nice, neat hair all wet, wouldn't we?"

"Cary, that's mean!" Jane looked hurt, and although he patted her shoulder by way of apology, her back remained stiff with anger. There *were* times (and this was definitely one of them) when Jane wished Cary had just one-tenth of Neal Worthington's class. Cornelius Worthington III, of the Boston Worthingtons, close friend of the Boston Barretts, had been her boyfriend until she met Cary. They were still good friends, and she still missed him. Especially during times like this, when Cary's determination to make her loosen up got in the way of his usual sensitivity.

Anyway, Neal wasn't interested in her in that way anymore. Not since he'd been introduced to a beautiful redhead from Texas. And isn't it funny, Jane thought, watching Toby, that the girl doesn't even *know* she's beautiful? But she *is*. Lucky Neal.

"No, it won't be Jane," Andy said firmly. "She's going to be too busy running things.

We need her organizational skills more than
we need to see her preppy clothes and nice,
neat hair all wet."

Jane sent her a silent thank-you look.

But Andy wasn't just defending her roommate. It was true. The Room 407 trio and
most of Baker House knew that Jane was super-
efficient at everything except keeping her part
of the room shipshape. She got her homework
in on time, returned her library books early,
and had already written most of the publicity
releases for the Almost Summer Carnival. So
they tolerated her section of the closet, which
was crammed-full from ceiling to floor with
shoes, belts, scarves, purses, and more clothes
than any human being could possibly need.
And they tolerated the mess around her bed,
an area that Andy suspected might be condemned by the Board of Health.

"I think the *boys* should volunteer for the
dunk tank," Jane said, still a little annoyed
with Cary. "They don't have to worry about
messing with their hair afterwards."

"*I* do," Cary reminded her with a grin.

"Well, go get it cut, then!" Jane snapped.

Cary laughed. He knew perfectly well that
although Jane had firm ideas about what was
socially acceptable and what wasn't, part of
his initial attraction for her was his being
different. Would she have paid the slightest
bit of attention to him if he'd looked like
every other guy she knew? No way. But then,
he probably wouldn't have been singing in a

rock group, either, and he wouldn't have run into her in the first place.

Matt Hall, sitting close to Andy, protested, "Hey, Jane, that's chauvinistic! Why should only the guys get dunked? It's your carnival, too."

Matt and Andy were an attractive pair. Taller than she, he moved with the same easy grace. He had been kind and helpful on more than one occasion, but had won Andy's undying loyalty by helping with the lighting at her dance recital. They had forged a common bond with their mutual interest in the entertainment world in general, dance and theater in particular. Unlike Jane and Cary, they had an easy, relaxed relationship that allowed a certain amount of good-natured give-and-take.

"Oh, Matt, relax," Andy teased, poking his arm gently. "Jane was just kidding."

"I was *not*!"

"Yes, you *were*. We females will do our share for this carnival, even if that includes being dunked. Now," Andy became businesslike once again, "who's going to volunteer to sign up volunteers for the dunk tank?"

"We will!" This came from Maggie Morrison and Dee Adams, occupants of Baker House's Room 409. A study in contrasts, Maggie was short and brown-haired, her roommate, a tall blonde California girl. They were friends as well as neighbors to the girls in 407.

As Andy jotted down their names on her list, a long-legged first-year girl in khaki shorts, a white shirt, and knee socks came striding across the lawn toward them. "Cord!" she called as she reached them, "you and your rommates are wanted in The Penthouse. Like right now."

The girls exchanged surprised glances. The Penthouse was the apartment at the top of Baker House occupied by their housemother, Meredith Pembroke. After a difficult start following Meredith's arrival, during which the new housemother had impersonated a drill sergeant and alienated the entire student body by tossing demerits around like confetti, things had straightened out. Admitting that she'd been overreacting to her own slightly wild adolescence, Meredith had finally relaxed. Now she treated them the way they'd been used to being treated by her predecessor, Allison, who had married and moved to Boston.

"Wonder what's up?" Jane murmured, getting to her feet. Andy and Toby did the same.

The girl shrugged. "Beats me. She just asked me to deliver the message." Giving them a mock salute, she said crisply, "Message delivered. See you."

As she turned and left, Cary said admiringly, "Cute!"

"I don't think I should leave him alone," Jane told Andy. "He can't be trusted. He might follow her."

"*Her*?" Cary exclaimed in mock horror.

"I'd never do that. She's not a Barrett. Good grief, she's not even from Boston!"

Andy and Toby quickly glanced at Jane, afraid she'd take offense at Cary's remarks. You never knew with Jane. Sometimes remarks about her background offended her, and sometimes she just laughed them off.

This time, she ignored Cary's remarks. She was wondering what Meredith wanted. "She probably just wants to see how we're doing on the carnival plans," she said aloud, as though reassuring herself. Turning to the others, still sitting on the ground, she said sternly, "You guys stay right here and keep on working. We'll be right back."

Another mock salute, this one from Cary. "Yes, ma'am, sergeant, sir!"

Laughing softly, Jane turned away. Her thoughts quickly returned to Meredith's summons. "Either of you two done anything you shouldn't have?"

Toby answered no right away, but Andy had to think about it for a minute. She never really *meant* to break rules. But sometimes they got in her way and before she knew it, wham! one broken rule. "Gee, I don't think so," she said slowly. Then she laughed. "We really are paranoid. The minute we know Meredith wants to see us, we start searching our brains for the crime we've committed. It's probably just the carnival she wants to talk about, right?"

"Right!" her roommates echoed. But they

kept right on searching their minds until Meredith opened The Penthouse door to them.

The expression on their housemother's normally cheerful face sent their hearts scurrying down into their sneakers (Andy's), Topsiders (Jane's), and cowboy boots (Toby's). There was no trace of a smile on Meredith's oval face. A tiny little furrow was etched across her forehead. That wasn't a good sign. The only time they saw that little line was when their housemother was concerned about something important.

"Sit down, girls," Merrie invited. "We need to talk."

Andy signaled Oh-oh with her eyes as she and her roommates sank to the thick white carpeting in front of the fireplace.

"Ms. Allardyce has asked me to give you a rather upsetting piece of news," Merrie said carefully, her voice quiet. "I'm afraid the Canby Hall maintenance crew has gone out on strike as of nine o'clock this morning."

Her guests continued to sit quietly, continued to give her their full attention. There was no visible reaction to her news from any of them.

Meredith decided that she hadn't made the situation clear to them. "All of the maintenance people," she said, "including the plumbers, electricians, carpenters, janitors and cleaning staff, and even most of the dining hall staff, have left campus."

Jane and Toby looked at each other, their faces blank. If Jane ever thought of the word *strike*, it was in terms of a baseball game. Toby's expression was every bit as blank as Jane's. The ranchhands who worked for her father were not part of any labor union.

Only Andy, whose parents owned and ran a restaurant in Chicago, understood. "Oh, no!" she cried while Toby and Jane stared at her. "Not *now*! What's the problem? Money, I suppose."

Meredith shook her head. Soft dark waves touched her cheek. "No. Not really. It's a cutback in working hours and pay. Dictated by the Board of Trustees. The workers say they can't finish their work in a shorter amount of time. So they've walked."

"Will someone," Jane demanded, "please tell me what on earth you're talking about?"

"But what about our carnival?" Andy asked Meredith, ignoring Jane's question. "How can we have our carnival without any maintenance people on campus? There's a lot of stuff that we don't know how to do. We *need* them!"

"That's just it," Meredith said softly, sympathy in her eyes. "I've just come from Ms. Allardyce's office. I'm afraid the carnival is off."

CHAPTER TWO

Andy, Jane, and Toby stared at their housemother in disbelief. "Off?" Andy croaked in horror. "You mean off as in canceled?"

Merrie nodded. "I'm sorry. Ms. Allardyce is trying to decide right now if she should close the school itself. How can she run a school without a staff?"

There was another brief stunned silence. Jane broke it by saying in an exasperated voice, "Well, this is just plain ridiculous! We've already done a lot of work on the carnival. And as for closing the school, well, Ms. Allardyce will just have to tell those people to get back to work. They can't just walk off the job like that!" Toby nodded agreement, but as Meredith and Andy continued to look grim, Jane added in a weaker voice, "*Can* they?"

Meredith sighed. "Yes, I'm afraid they can, Jane. They originally agreed to work a certain number of hours. Now the Board of Trustees, in an attempt to save money, is telling the workers they have to do the same amount of work in less time." She shrugged. "They say it just can't be done. They're very angry."

"I don't want to go home just now," Toby said quietly, surprising all of them. She had been homesick for Texas for so long. No one had expected this particular remark from this particular person. She blushed. "I'm just beginning to see how really pretty spring in New England can be," she explained. And although she didn't add that Texas was "mighty far" away from Neal Worthington, Jane sensed that Toby was thinking just that. That romance was just getting off the ground. This was no time to be heading for Texas.

"None of us want to go home just now," Andy said just a bit impatiently. "We want our carnival! Can't you do anything?" she begged Meredith.

Meredith spread her hands helplessly in front of her. "What can I do? Ms. Allardyce is right. She can't run Canby Hall without help. There's too much work involved in keeping it going.

"*We* can do it!" Andy sat up straighter.

"Oh-oh," Jane muttered to Toby, "she's got that look in her eyes. Watch out!"

Before Meredith could say anything, Andy had jumped to her feet. "Why not? It's just things like cleaning and laundry, stuff like that, isn't it? That absolutely has to be done, I mean? That other stuff: The plumbing and electricity, that sort of stuff only pops up once in a while, right? I mean, my dad only calls a plumber or an electrician when he has a problem he can't fix himself."

"Andy. . . ."

Andy waved away Meredith's warning. "No, listen, *we* can cook and do laundry. We can even help out in the dining hall. Jane and Toby and I all have experience."

Jane made a choking sound. The experience Andy was talking about had been a brief visit to Chicago where the three of them had helped out in the Cord family restaurant. As far as she was concerned, that was an experience she didn't want to repeat.

"Andy, slow down!" Meredith commanded. "You just don't realize what's involved here."

Andy stopped talking. But the determined expression on her face remained.

"First of all," their housemother said patiently, "there is an incredible amount of work involved in running Canby Hall. That's the whole point of the strike. Surely you can see that."

Andy nodded politely. Canby Hall covered a large area of ground. There were dorms and other buildings, such as the Administration Building, the Library, and the Dining Hall, to be taken care of. There were walkways crisscrossing the campus that would need sweeping, the pond and the wishing well would need cleaning, the new green of the expanses of lawn would need mowing. "Yes," she said. "If there wasn't so much to do, the staff wouldn't *mind* having their hours cut."

Meredith looked pleased. "Right! Secondly, they're striking to prove how necessary they are. If you girls took on many of their duties, how could they get their point across? They wouldn't take kindly to any interference on your part."

Some of the excitement left Andy's dark eyes. "I hadn't thought of that." Then she cheered up. "Oh, gosh, Merrie, we're not really going to be replacing anyone. We don't know enough to do that. We'll just . . . well, hold their jobs open for them. Isn't that what it would be? After all," she added sensibly, "if Canby Hall closes, they won't have any jobs to come back to, right?"

Meredith looked doubtful.

Andy smiled. "Good! Great! Okay, you two," turning to her stunned roommates, "what we need to do right now is go break the news to the gang. And make them promise to help. Then we have to sit down and make up chore charts to take to P.A. when we tackle her." Realizing she'd used their nickname for the headmistress, Andy glanced quickly at their housemother, but Meredith didn't seem to care.

Jane frowned. "Chore charts?" A Barrett was as familiar with the concept of chores as she was with the concept of labor strikes, which was not at all.

"Yes, Jane, chore charts. Duty assignments.

You know — a list of who does what when. So we can keep Canby Hall open and have our carnival." Andy's eyes narrowed. "You do intend to help, don't you?"

If Canby Hall closed and Jane went home to Boston, where the household help had never gone on strike and in all likelihood never would, there would be no chore charts for her to face. There would also be no Cary Slade and no carnival. "Of course I'm going to help," she said indignantly. "It's my school, too. I just thought, well, I sort of thought I'd be in *charge*. Of the charts, I mean." That way she could decide which chores would be the least repulsive and maybe sign up for them first.

Andy grinned. "You mean you're better at assigning chores than doing them? Jane, we all know that. But this time I think everyone's going to have to pitch in. Including you. You can wear rubber gloves to protect those aristocratic hands of yours while you're scrubbing the bathroom."

Jane paled. Scrubbing? The bathroom?

"I'll help, too," Toby offered. "But I've gotta tell you, Andy, I don't know a whole heck of a lot about cleaning and cooking, either. We've always had someone at the ranch to do that stuff. I worked outside, mostly."

"That's okay. There'll be outside stuff to do, too. The maintenance people were always on the grounds somewhere. You can find out what it was they were doing, and do it."

Toby seemed pleased with that idea.

With Meredith's doubtful good wishes, they left the apartment and hurried back down the stairs and outside.

Although everyone was shocked by their news, they all agreed to help, even the boys from Oakley Prep. Using Magic Markers and enlisting the aid of girls from the two other dorms, Andy began the chore charts. Each House, they decided, would be run separately, staffed by its own residents. The Dining Hall would have to be run cooperatively, with girls from all three dorms taking turns cleaning up, doing dishes, even cooking if necessary.

Jane's eyes widened in horror at the last suggestion. That week in the Cord restaurant would be a piece of cake compared to getting a meal ready for her fellow students. The week in Chicago had left her with aching feet and back, a sharp dent in her self-confidence, and, for a while, a very short temper. A week in the dining hall would almost certainly kill her.

"I will help clean the dining hall," she said. "I will even do dishes, if I absolutely must. But if anyone makes me cook, the infirmary will be stacked to the rafters with bodies, I promise."

Cary laughed. "That bad, eh? Remind me to turn down any dinner invitations from you when we're back in Boston."

Jane stared at him. "Why? *I* don't do any cooking in Boston."

Everyone laughed. Cary laughed loudest of all.

When the charts were finished, Andy volunteered the 407 girls to approach Ms. Allardyce. When Jane and Toby hesitated, Andy said "piece of cake" confidently, and they agreed to accompany her to what Jane called "the lion's den."

When Maggie expressed doubt about their errand, Andy scolded her. "Where's your faith?" she asked, only half-kidding. "Besides, we've got our charts." She held them up in front of her. The bold Magic Marker lines and squares clashed violently with her pale pink sweater. "How can Ms. Allardyce say no to these?"

"Are you kidding?" Maggie said. "She's the headmistress. She can say no to anything she wants to."

Andy smiled. "That's just the point. She can't *want* to close Canby Hall. So she'll be relieved that we've figured all this out, right?"

When no one answered, Matt took pity on her. Putting an arm around her shoulders, he said, "It can't hurt to try. And if anyone can talk Ms. Allardyce into something, it's our girl here. C'mon, everyone, wish this trio good luck."

The group gave in at Matt's urging, and the three girls and their cardboard charts were followed by shouts of "Good luck!" and "Go get 'er!" as they walked away. It helped a little.

Knowing Ms. Allardyce wouldn't be at home when there was a crisis on campus, they went straight to her office. Her secretary showed them in.

Andy had said Ms. Allardyce would be relieved to see their charts and hear about their wonderful idea. Stunned would have been a better word.

"Let me get this straight," the tall, gray-suited woman said, standing behind her desk and surveying the group with cool blue eyes. "You intend to run Canby Hall?"

"Oh, no, ma'am," Andy said hastily. "We just want to help." Holding up the charts, she continued, "We have plenty of volunteers already, and we'll get lots more. Nobody wants the school closed."

"Nor do I," their headmistress said. Jane wondered idly how she managed to keep her hair in that beautiful French twist. Taking the charts from Andy, Ms. Allardyce placed them flat on her desk. "These are very interesting. But I fail to see how you girls can do all of this and still keep up with your studies."

Alarmed, the three girls stepped forward as one person. "We've thought of that," Jane said, pointing toward the charts. "That's why the assignments are staggered. So we'll all have enough study time."

Ms. Allardyce looked skeptical. But she continued to study the charts. They all knew she was searching for an answer to her problem. Closing a private school down before the term had ended could finish the school forever.

Sometimes Toby surprised her roommates. This was one of those times. Stepping forward, she drawled, "Ms. Allardyce, it's just that we sure don't want our education interrupted. We'd have to make up the time this summer, and nobody wants to go to school when it's real hot. If y'all could see your way clear to keeping Canby Hall open, we'd work like mules, and that's a promise."

Amusement glinted in the headmistress's eyes as Jane and Andy nodded agreement. "Well," she said, "I know very little about mules, but I can't disagree with your motives. Your education is, of course, foremost in my mind. I'm just a bit surprised that it is in yours as well."

"Oh, yes, Ms. Allardyce," Andy said, "it *is*! We just couldn't stand it if — "

The headmistress interrupted with a raised hand. "Don't overstate your case, Andrea," she said dryly. "You might convince me that canceling your carnival wouldn't even raise an eyebrow, since it has little to do with education."

Three faces tried hard to look innocent.

"No," she said quickly, "we needn't do that just yet. I know you've already done a great deal of work on it. For now, I'll withhold a decision on the event."

Ms. Allardyce hesitated. Then she said, "All right." She tapped the charts with one finger. "We'll give your plan a try." Sighing, she added, "I hope I'm not making a terrible mistake here. At this point, I'm willing to try anything.

"But," she added quickly as she handed the charts back to them, "this is all on a trial basis. You must be aware of that. I suspect you may be biting off more than you can chew. At the very *first* sign of trouble, I will be forced to call off this experiment and, of course, your carnival, immediately. Is that understood?"

Andy tucked the charts under her arm. Nodding, she said soberly, "Yes, Ms. Allardyce. Don't worry, there won't be any trouble. And thanks. Thanks a lot!"

The headmistress gave them a smile. "Yes, well, I must say it *is* nice to know that you girls feel the same way I do about Canby Hall." She led them to the door and opened it. "Just be very careful, please. Do not do anything you're not absolutely sure you can do, and come to me the moment you change your mind about all of this."

Promising to do just that and thanking her again, they left.

In high spirits, they ran back to the group on campus. "We did it!" Andy cried, tossing the charts on the ground and throwing her arms around Matt. "She's going to keep the school open!"

"And for right now, at least, the carnival is still on!" Jane added happily, grabbing Cary's hand.

There was a lot of cheering, shouting, and congratulations for the triumphant trio. When they had taken seats on the ground, Jane said nervously. "Now all we have to do is follow through." Her blue eyes traveled across the charts lying on the ground. "That looks like an awful lot of work."

Andy laughed. "*Any* kind of housework would look like a lot to you."

"Well, that's true enough," Jane admitted with a grin. "But I'm a Barrett," she added proudly, "and we always do our best. And *this* Barrett will be right there in the trenches with everybody else."

"Trenches? Trenches?" Andy scanned the charts with mock interest. "I don't see any ditch-digging on these charts."

Instead of answering, Jane jumped up and grabbed a water balloon prepared for the dart booth. Popping it with a stick she found on the ground, she let the water cascade over Andy's dark hair.

Shrieking as cold water hit her face, Andy jumped up to retaliate. The balloon she grabbed was blue. Then Cary yanked a yellow one out of the pile of filled balloons, while Toby, laughing, reached for a green one.

And the water balloon battle was on.

CHAPTER THREE

Now we have to blow up another package of balloons and fill them," Jane scolded when everyone was thoroughly and happily wet. "We've just made more work for ourselves. I don't think we're starting off on the right foot here."

"Jane," Andy said mildly, "who broke the first balloon?"

"What?" Jane thought for a minute and then, remembering, she laughed sheepishly. "Oh. Sorry."

"Listen, we'll do everything we can to help, okay?" Cary said. "We don't want Canby to close, either, for lots of reasons, the carnival just being one of them." Jane's cheeks reddened. "But can we at least walk into the village for pizza before we put our noses to the grindstone?"

"No," Jane answered firmly. All of her companions moaned in disappointment. "We have to make copies of these chore charts right now.

This minute. Enough copies for everyone at Canby Hall. That's going to take a while. We'll just have to endure Hell's Kitchen later instead of having pizza."

She was referring to the Dining Hall, where no prizes for culinary genius would be awarded by the students who ate there. Which was one reason most Saturdays involved a trip to the village for what Andy called credible edibles.

This Saturday wasn't one of them. "We have to start this schedule first thing tomorrow morning," Jane pointed out. "That doesn't give us a whole lot of time to spread the word about what we're doing. And to hand out assignments."

"Well," Andy said as she bent to pick up some of the carnival supplies, "since the staff just left campus today, there shouldn't be that much to do tomorrow. We can probably get a lot done on the carnival before things get too hectic." Turning to Matt, she asked, "So can you guys show up tomorrow right after lunch?"

He nodded. "There isn't anything we can do to help tonight?" Then he added more quickly, "I guess this means our movie date is off, hmm?"

Andy nodded sadly as Jane said crisply, "No, you can't help tonight. It's mostly organization right now and guys are no good at that."

"Hey," Cary protested, "that's garbage!

This is *our* carnival, too, and we've done as much organizing as you girls have."

That was true. Many of the good ideas had come from the Oakley Prep students.

"Maybe," Jane admitted. "But it's *our* school we're trying to keep open, so *we* should be in charge. If we need your help, we'll call you." She gave Cary a quick kiss on the cheek. "See you tomorrow."

Jane was right. Making and distributing enough copies of the chore charts took a long time. They had worked through the dinner hour. No one minded. Thanks to the constant generosity of Andy's parents, Room 407 never went hungry. Now, collapsed in their room, they watched Andy drag a box out from underneath her bed. Everyone dug into crackers, cheese spread, apples, and frosted brownies thick with nuts.

Relaxed and happy with the mini-feast, each girl got comfortable in her own section of the room while she ate. The individuality of each little area was a tribute to the individuality of the girls themselves.

If Jane had been neater, her part of the room would have been beautiful. As it was, the cross-stitch quilt fought constantly with a collection of discarded clothing, books, notebooks, and make-up. The pastel Persian rug on the floor beside her bed was often hidden by shoes, boots, magazines, and half-eaten bags of potato chips or discarded apple cores. The old-fashioned milk-glass lamp on her nightstand cast its glow on soda cans, hair-brushes, more books and notebooks, and a dozen small objects.

Andy's section was both less sophisticated and much neater than Jane's. Ballet posters on the wall told more about her than anything else in the corner. Lop-eared and faded stuffed animals on the geometric patterned, earth-toned bedspread were evidence of Andy's strong sense of loyalty. Any friend she made was a friend for life — including stuffed animals. Several of her frequent letters from home lay opened on her nightstand. A jump-rope she sometimes used for fitness exercise, which drove the occupants of Room 307 crazy, lay curled at the foot of her neatly made bed. Hers was a warm, attractive little corner.

Toby's part of the room had improved the most since her arrival. A rainbow-striped spread had finally replaced the green Army blanket. A matching throw rug further bright-ened the area. But the only decorations were a two-sided picture frame on her desk with photographs of a lean, unsmiling Jed Hous-ton, Toby's father, on one side and her horse Max on the other. A tea bag hung, without explanation, over her bed.

"Don't you want that tea bag in rainbow stripes, too?" Andy had teased as Toby was making the bed with the new spread. She was hoping Toby would explain the bizarre ac-cessory.

"Nope. It's just fine the way it is." And that was that.

Less than five minutes after they had all settled on their beds, they had their first argument about the strike.

"What a pain this is!" Jane complained as she bent over the chore charts for Baker House. "You'd think people would have more sense than to walk off their jobs."

Andy's head shot up. "Are you serious? You heard what Merrie said. Those trustees want the workers to cut back on their hours. That's not fair."

Jane frowned. "Why isn't it? Couldn't they just work faster? They've probably been wasting time, and maybe that's why the Board made this decision."

Andy slapped her apple core down on her notebook. "Honestly, Jane! It's just like you to put the blame on working people. I suppose just because the Board members are probably all people like your mom and dad, you think they can do no wrong."

"Hey, you guys, cut it out!" Toby called.

They ignored her. "This doesn't have a single thing to do with my father or my mother," Jane said coldly. "People who are hired to do a job should just do it, that's all."

Toby nodded. "She's got a point, Andy. I mean, everyone on the ranch has tons of stuff to do. That's just the way it is, so they do it. If a hand does leave, my dad just hires another hand."

"Well, maybe cowboys are different from regular people," Andy snapped. She was hurt by Toby's disloyalty. She had expected it from Jane. What did Jane know about working for a living? But Toby, like Andy, wasn't rich. She had known people who worked for a living all of her life. And Andy had counted on support from her. "Regular people can't afford to just go from job to job. They have to stick up for their rights on the job they already have."

"Cowboys *are* regular people," Toby defended. She'd thought she was making progress convincing everyone that Texas wasn't an alien planet. Andy's remarks hurt.

Andy sensed her mistake. "I'm sorry, Tobe," she apologized. "But you've got to admit most of your ranchhands are single. You said yourself some of them are drifters. The people who work here are mostly married and have families. They live right in the village. They can't just pick up and leave." She glowered at Jane. "You just don't understand what it's like to have to work really hard for a living."

Thoroughly irritated, Jane said sarcastically, "Oh, and you do? Are you or are you not sitting at this very moment on a bed in a very expensive private school?"

An embarrassed look spread across Andy's smooth face. "Well, I — "

"Listen," Toby interrupted anxiously, "why

don't we declare a truce? We have got to get going on these chore charts for Baker House, or nothing's going to get done. We start tomorrow, guys, and it's already late."

Disgruntled but aware that she was right, her roommates nodded. Making copies of the charts wouldn't do any good if they didn't fill them in with each assignment and who was going to do it.

"The girls at Addison and Charles are probably already finished with their charts," Toby added. "We should be done, too, and we haven't even started."

"All right," Jane said briskly, taking the list of names of Baker House residents in one hand, and the chore chart for the House in the other, "let's get this over with. You guys get the Dining Hall duty tomorrow. See if you can sabotage the menu and substitute something edible, okay?"

Toby's eyes grew very large. "We won't have to cook, will we?"

Jane shook her long blonde hair. "Probably not. Two of the cooks are staying on." She grinned. "Can't take more than two cooks to spoil the broth in Hell's Kitchen, right?" Then she looked up at Toby. "Why? I thought you said you cooked sometimes out there in No-Man's Land."

Toby shrugged. "Just bacon and eggs. Sometimes stew. Stuff like that. I never did much real cooking."

Andy laughed. "Real cooking? You mean you never cooked up a mess of brown stuff or green stuff or gray stuff?"

Laughing, Toby relaxed.

"You'll be doing clean-up," Jane said, making notations on her chart. "That's going to be the toughest part, keeping the Dining Hall and the dorms clean. P.A. has an eagle eye. If she spots grease and grime anywhere, we'll be on our way home before we can say 'Ms. Clean.' "

"Speaking of which," Andy said, shifting into Indian position on her bed, "do we know where to find the cleaning junk we'll need? You know, all that spray stuff in cans and bottles and some paper towels?"

"Fourth floor broom closet," Jane reminded her briskly. They were all familiar with the little room. It served two purposes. Besides house-cleaning equipment, it had become the best refuge for a student craving privacy. Each of them had occasionally shed a private tear or two in among the mops and pails, brooms and brushes and bottles.

Andy nodded. "Right. I forgot. Jane, what are you going to tackle tomorrow? Linens? Floors? Bathrooms?"

Jane's face went a shade paler. "Me?" She avoided Andy's eyes, bending her head toward the chart. "I'm . . . well, I'm organizing. Doesn't that count for something? I'll have to keep these charts updated and make sure everyone does what they're supposed to. That takes time."

"Meredith can do that."

"I still have the carnival to work on."

"So do we," Andy said calmly, her dark brown eyes narrowing. "Jane, you are planning on helping out with the dirty work, aren't you? I mean, we're all in this together, right?"

Jane sighed and nodded reluctantly. "I'm just going to be so busy," she complained.

Andy stood up. "Jane," she said firmly, "everyone is going to be just as busy as you are. But you were right there with us when we promised P.A. that we'd keep this school open. Now put your name down right there beside fourth floor bathroom number one."

Jane looked up, her lovely face the color of oatmeal. "Bathroom?" she echoed weakly.

Andy nodded, a mischievous glint in her eyes. "The one *we* use. Put Maggie or Dee down for the other one. One bathroom won't take you all that long."

"But . . . I mean, well, why *me*? There are a lot of other girls who could do it."

"You've never in your life cleaned a bathroom before, have you, Jane?"

Mutely, Jane shook her head. "But I'll bet," she said angrily, "that there are other girls in Baker House who haven't, either." Her tone changed to one of bewilderment. "Why *would* they?"

Toby laughed, and Andy relented. The

steely edge in her voice disappeared. Crouching down beside Jane's bed, balancing her dancer's body perfectly, she said, "Look, Jane, it'll be a new experience. Isn't that what writers are always looking for? You may need to write about someone cleaning a bathroom one day, and now you'll know what to say about the experience."

"I don't," Jane replied loftily, "intend to write about bathrooms. Not ever! Who would read it?"

"People who clean bathrooms," Andy answered matter-of-factly. "They're out there, Jane. Trust me."

Toby laughed. Jane just shrugged. "Well, you both may have done your share of housekeeping, but I've always counted on hired help to keep things in order."

Her roommates glanced at the mountain of clutter on and around her bed. "Yeah, we figured," Toby said. "Listen, you guys really think we can pull this off?"

"Oh, sure," Andy said airily, dismissing Toby's doubts with a wave of her hand. "We can do anything. I bet," with a grin, "we can even teach Jane which way to point the spray cleaner."

"We'd better," Toby agreed as Jane glared in mock anger. "Or we'll walk into the bathroom tomorrow and find five feet, four inches of solid cleaning foam and no Jane."

That image sent them all into gales of laughter.

CHAPTER FOUR

Sunday did not begin well. The laughter of the night before was forgotten quickly as grim reality set in. The girls of Room 407 had worked on their chore charts long after lights out with the help of Toby's trusty old flashlight. As a result, Toby and Andy both woke up with headaches and Jane was, as Toby put it, "as cross as a rabbit stuck in a briar patch."

"What a rotten way to start the day," Andy moaned as she pulled on jeans and a bright yellow T-shirt with the words "DANCE OR DIE TRYING" emblazoned on the front. "We shouldn't have stayed up so late."

"We *had* to," Jane reminded her. She selected a pair of soft gray trousers and a gray and peach crew-neck sweater from her bulging closet. "We had to get those stupid charts done."

"Those 'stupid charts,' " a jean-clad Toby said quietly as she buttoned a plaid blouse, "are going to help us keep this school open."

"Not if we don't get busy and do what's *on* those 'stupid charts,'" Andy pointed out. "Jane, you've got to be kidding."

"About what?"

"Those clothes! You're going to be cleaning, not taking a stroll across campus with a gorgeous guy. Put on some ratty old things." The minute the words left her mouth, she grinned. "Ratty clothes? Jane? Am I crazy or what? Well, find the oldest clothes you've got and throw them on."

Jane hesitated. Old clothes? Why would she have *old* clothes? Why would anyone keep old clothes? And even if she had wanted to keep them, there wasn't room in her closet for anything but the things she'd bought for this term.

Seeing her hesitation, Andy lost her patience. "Jane! We're all going to be late. Just grab something. After all, if you ruin it, it's not as if you'll be forced to run around in a towel. You'll probably be able to find *something* to wear in your closet."

Jane settled on a bright pink sweatshirt, worn only once, because she felt it didn't complement her complexion.

"C'mon," Andy urged, "I'll show you what you need for the bathroom work. Meet us in the Dining Hall when you're done. Toby, you knock on doors and hand out those assignments for this week."

Toby made a face. Waking people up early on a Sunday morning to give them work to do wasn't going to make her very popular. Good thing she didn't care all that much. Being Ms. Popularity just wasn't one of her major goals in life. Following in her father's footsteps, however, was. She wanted to be a rancher one day. It could be lonely; she knew that. If she needed, as many of the girls seemed to, to be surrounded by people, ranching would be the last career she'd choose.

Still, she didn't especially like having people mad at her, either. And as she strode from room to room in Baker House, the heels of her cowboy boots clicking on the shiny hardwood floors, she began to wish again that this strike was just a bad dream. The moaning and groaning from half-asleep fellow students annoyed her.

She'd never seen so many wimps in her life!

But they all agreed (sleepily) to get dressed and get busy. Hoping they meant it, Toby hurried back to meet Andy and head for the Dining Hall. Her curly red hair flew as she strode down the hall.

As Andy and Toby hurried across campus, Jane stood in the middle of the all-white bathroom, a yellow plastic bucket full of supplies hanging on one arm and an expression of bewilderment on her face.

Before she could decide on her first step, Dee arrived with a thick white towel over her shoulders. She was carrying a shampoo bottle and a hairbrush in one hand. "Hi, Jane, what's up?"

"I'm . . ." Jane's upper lip curled, "I'm going to clean in here."

Dee shook her head emphatically. Sun-streaked hair flew around her face. "Oh, no, you're not! Not now. You have to do that later, after everyone's had their shower." Footsteps sounded in the hall outside. "Hear that? That's the sound of the troops arriving for their morning ablutions. Get in their way, you'll get trampled."

"But. . . ." Jane felt a mixture of relief and impatience. She wouldn't mind at all putting off the stupid chore. On the other hand, it might be better just to get it out of the way. Then maybe she could hurry back to her room and hide under the covers for the rest of the day.

The decision was taken out of her hands as a horde of sleepy, cranky girls descended upon the bathroom.

"This is dumb!" Jane tried. "Why take a shower now? You're all just going to get dirty doing all those chores."

No one listened to her. So, telling herself that it wasn't *her* fault, she headed, bucket still on her arm, back to Room 407. She wasn't hungry enough to go to the Dining Hall and besides, if she did, Andy would surely start cracking a whip over her head. Wasn't she entitled to a tiny little nap? Hadn't she stayed up half the night working on those charts?

Repeating to herself several times that it wasn't *her* fault she couldn't clean the bathroom just now, Jane slapped her bucket down on the floor beside her bed and crawled under her comforter. She was asleep in seconds.

While Jane slept blissfully, Andy and Toby were being painfully introduced to the routine in the Dining Hall.

"Whew!" Andy said breathlessly as she hauled a large tray full of dirty dishes to the kitchen, "I could use about six more hands!"

"Yeah, me, too," Toby agreed. She was crouching down, scraping a pile of scrambled eggs from the floor. Unfortunately for her, they'd been stepped on before she'd reached them, which made her job more difficult.

"I thought this would be like working in my father's restaurant, didn't you? That wasn't so bad, was it? This is worse!"

Toby said nothing. That week they'd gone to Chicago to help in the Cord family restaurant had been an adventure and she wasn't sorry they'd gone. But it hadn't been easy, waitressing. It was hard work.

"I think this is harder," Andy elaborated. "The kitchen equipment is so out-dated. There aren't enough trays, either. And none of the other girls helping seems to have ever cooked for more than two."

Toby stood up, tray full of mashed scrambled egg in hand. Brushing a stray red curl out of her eyes, she sighed. "Did you see the toast Maggie made? It looked like barbecued cardboard."

Andy giggled. "Joyce Miller said she was going to use hers for a place mat."

Toby wiped her perspiring face with a napkin. "I wonder where Jane is? Shouldn't she be here by now?"

Andy rolled her eyes heavenward. "She's probably being held captive by a runaway mop." She grinned. "Or maybe she just hasn't figured out how to get the top off the foam spray cleaner can. How do rich kids survive in the real world?"

As Toby entered the kitchen, she was confronted by a two-inch thick layer of billowing soapsuds on the floor in front of the dishwasher. Two very disgusted cooks were carefully edging around the suds to avoid slipping on the wet floor. "Honestly," one of them said as she handed Toby a mop, "I hope you girls aren't going to harm more than you help." Her partner added quickly, "We know you mean well, but you're not being very helpful." Shaking her head, she returned to the stove, muttering to herself something about "In *my* day. . . ."

Toby attacked the suds, assisted by the embarrassed first-year student who had overloaded the dishwasher's soap container. "I'm sorry," she mumbled. "Really. I feel like such a jerk."

Toby had felt exactly the same way the first night she'd helped in the Cord restaurant. "That's okay," she said generously. "Did you see the toast Maggie made?" The girl nodded and managed a grin. "Look at it this way," Toby added, pushing her mop across the floor. "We're here for an education, right? Well, we're certainly getting one today. We're learning Everything Nobody Ever Wanted to Know About Breakfast at Canby Hall. I'm just glad we're not being graded on any of this."

Andy popped her head in to announce that she was going to run back to Baker House and see if Jane had been overwhelmed and ran away from school. Toby nodded and went on mopping.

At Baker House, Andy went straight to bathroom number one and walked into chaos. There were wet towels everywhere, some hanging on shower stall doors, some in sodden heaps on the floor, a few lying on the long, narrow vanity. Soggy soap bars clung to corners of sinks, crumpled tissues overflowed from the wastebasket.

The first thought that struck her was, Has everyone at Canby always been so disgustingly sloppy? Did I just not notice because the staff cleaned up after us?

Her second thought was, WHERE IS JANE?

She had no trouble finding her missing roommate. To Andy's complete disgust, there

Jane was, sleeping the morning away while everyone else worked their fingers to the bone. Andy was as disappointed as she was angry. True, Jane Barrett was more than a little spoiled, and sometimes unbearably snobbish. But she wasn't lazy and she wasn't a shirker. Everyone knew Jane could be counted on. She was considered reliable by everyone who knew her.

Andy wasn't very gentle about waking her up. "Jane! Jane Barrett, you wake up this very minute!"

Jane jerked awake with a start. Guilt flooded her face the instant she saw Andy standing over her. She sat up. "Oh, gosh, what time is it?"

"Ten-thirty," she grimly stated. "What's the big idea? The bathroom looks like a herd of elephants got trapped in there and had to fight their way out."

"I'm sorry," Jane said honestly, "I really am. But it wasn't my fault."

Andy made a rude sound.

"No, listen! I can't clean it first thing in the morning because that's when everyone needs to get in there. So I had to wait. And then, well, I decided to wait in here, and I sat down on the bed, and . . ."

"And you couldn't possibly have come on over to the Dining Hall to help us out while you waited." Andy's voice was full of disgust.

Jane jumped out of bed. "I'll do the bathroom right now. I just meant to take the tiniest little nap. I guess I was just worn out from last night."

"Yeah, aren't we all." Andy fixed a level gaze on Jane. "You sure it's safe to leave you alone? I've got to get back to the Dining Hall."

Jane's flush deepened. "Yes, you can trust me. By the time you get back, the bathroom will look like an operating room, I promise."

Andy nodded doubtfully and left. Jane picked up the yellow pail and headed straight for the bathroom. I'm a Barrett, she reminded herself, smoothing down her sleep-rumpled hair, and I *can* do this.

That determination evaporated like mist on the bathroom mirror when she saw the mess. Oh, good grief, she thought, is this some sort of test? A What Does It Take to Lick a Barrett test?

Well, she thought grimly, rolling up the sleeves of her sweatsuit top, I'm *not* flunking!

Easier said than done. What was she supposed to do with the wet towels? Were they just hung up to dry and be reused (she shuddered), or should they go directly to the laundry? Following her own preference, she collected the towels and dumped them outside the door. She'd take them to the laundry when she'd finished pulling this place back together.

Where did all that trash falling out of the wastebasket go? Andy hadn't told her. She had nothing to put any trash in. She finally settled for stomping the trash down with her foot and sticking the basket outside the door with the wet towels. She'd deal with the trash later, too. There! She'd already accomplished a great deal. All it really took was a certain amount of intelligence. Anyone could clean a bathroom. She'd be finished here in no time at all.

The first thing she did wrong was aim the glass cleaner toward herself, forgetting Andy's warning against doing that very thing. Luckily, she had been aiming at the bottom of the mirror, not the top. Only her sweatsuit top got wet, not her face or eyes. Then the mirror seemed to stretch on forever. It had to be the longest mirror in the entire universe. It traveled from one end of the room to the other, and every inch of it had to be sprayed and wiped.

Her roll of paper towels slipped out of her hands, landing in a sink half-full of water because the drain was clogged with wet tissues. Jane snarled in a way that was decidedly un-Barrett-like.

Substituting damp bath towels for the useless paper roll, she tried again. But wiping the mirror with damp towels created a trail of lint across the glass. Giving up, she hurried out to the broom closet for another roll of paper towels.

Cleaning the sinks seemed to take forever. Who needed all these sinks, anyway? Why couldn't the girls just take turns? It wasn't until she got to the fifth sink that she realized she was still using the window cleaner instead of the foam cleaner Andy had recommended. No wonder they didn't look all that clean. Switching wearily from bottle to can, she began again.

At the last sink, her elbow bumped a mushy bar of soap, sending it to the floor. Although her eyes never saw it go, her foot quickly located it. Jane went flying, landing on her back on a floor that still hadn't been mopped free of puddles. It was either laugh or cry. Taking a deep breath, she laughed. When she had finished laughing, she got up, picked up her mop, and began cleaning the floor.

"No time at all" turned out to be a shocking one hour and forty minutes. She couldn't believe it when, exhausted and sweating, she glanced at her watch. She also noticed two broken fingernails, every bit as distressing to her as the length of time it had taken to clean the bathroom. The tiniest trace of empathy for the striking employees tugged at the edges of her mind. After all, they not only had to do this one bathroom, they had to do all of the bathrooms in Baker House, and more besides. Dismissing the trace of empathy because she didn't want to feel it, she headed for the broom closet.

CHAPTER FIVE

A group of boys from Oakley Prep descended upon the campus that Sunday afternoon. Wearing what Jane disdainfully called "scuzz" clothes, they came prepared to work on the carnival.

"It's a great day!" Cary said, smiling down at an exhausted and very cranky Jane. "We can get a lot done this afternoon."

"I've *already* done a lot!" Jane complained, sinking down on the lawn beside the stone wishing well, where they had all gathered. "So just don't expect much from me, okay?"

Cary's thin face registered sympathy. "Rough, huh?" He bent to deliver a swift kiss. "It'll get easier, you'll see. Hard work never killed anybody."

"That's ridiculous. Hard work has killed lots of people."

"Listen, guys," Andy interrupted. She stood in the center of their circle. "We've got trouble."

"So what else is new?" Matt asked. He was standing beside her. If she hadn't been so distracted, it would have crossed her mind that he looked great in an old blue sweatshirt, sleeves pushed up to the elbow. But Andy had more important things on her mind.

"I've been going over the carnival notes from last year." She held up a thick black looseleaf notebook. "And I've got bad news." Always dramatic, she paused to let that sink in. "All of the carnival booths have always been built by the maintenance crew."

No one said anything. But she still had their undivided attention.

"So *we* have to build them. Or go without."

"Don't be silly," Dee piped up with a light laugh. "We don't know the first thing about building booths." She looked around the circle. "*Do* we?"

"But we have to have booths," Maggie protested, her round eyes full of dismay behind wire-rimmed glasses. "We need them for the popcorn and cotton candy, for the cold drinks, for the ring toss and the water balloon dart board and — "

"We know that, Maggie," Dee interrupted impatiently. "And the dunk tank has to have that round wooden tub around it, too. Andy? Aren't you in charge of the dunk tank?"

Andy nodded grimly.

"Well," Dee persisted, "does anyone here

have the slightest idea how you build a round wooden frame for a dunk tank?"

"It doesn't *have* to be round," Toby said thoughtfully. "Round is too hard for beginners. We'll just make it the same shape as the other booths only bigger. Just large enough so the metal dunking tank will fit inside it. That's the tank that's in the basement at Baker, right, Andy?"

Andy nodded. She'd already checked. The tank was there, all right, but it would look really ugly without a wooden frame around it.

Discouraged, she glanced across campus to where a line of workers carrying signs walked slowly past the Administration Building. Maybe Jane was right. Maybe they shouldn't have just walked off the job like that.

Then, ashamed of herself for being angry with the workers now that what she wanted was being threatened, she said quickly, "We'll figure something out. I mean, anything we make doesn't have to win the Frank Lloyd Wright award for design, does it?"

"Who's Frank Lloyd Wright?" Maggie wanted to know.

Ignoring her, Carey said, "Andy's right. We slap a few boards together, hammer in some nails and presto! We've got booths."

"Right!" Jane agreed, anxious to get on with this meeting and dash to her bed where she could rest her weary body. "We'll show those maintenance people we can do just fine without them!"

Cary's expression told her she'd said the wrong thing. "Jane," he scolded with a stern frown, "that's *not* what we're trying to do here. The workers are well within their rights, and I support them. I'm not interested in teaching them a lesson. The thing is, Oakley and Canby have a carnival to put on. With the strike on, we just have to do it ourselves, that's all I'm saying. You guys know where the tools are kept?"

Jane looked at him in disgust. When had *he* ever cleaned a bathroom? "Tools?"

"Yeah, you know: hammer, nails, saw, that kind of stuff. If you think it's hard to build booths without the maintenance staff, just try it without tools."

"They're probably in the basement," Andy offered. "We could check there. If there aren't any there, Merrie might know where they are."

The girls who had staffed the Dining Hall during lunch arrived. "Personally," a blonde girl with a dark smudge on one cheek said, "I think P.A. had the right idea in the first place. Closing the school would have given everyone a nice little vacation. Instead, we're slaving away like scullery workers."

"What's a scullery?" Maggie asked.

"Maggie, go find a dictionary!" Dee said in exasperation.

Shaking their heads, the Dining Hall girls left the group.

Andy looked alarmed. "Gee, I hope no one else feels like that. We need all the help we can get."

Matt tried to cheer her up. "Don't worry about it. Let's take one thing at a time. Right now, we need to find those tools. Take me to your cellar, Miss!"

"I'm a Ms. not a Miss," she corrected. But she led him to the basement in Baker House.

They found the tools without any trouble, hanging on a pegboard along one wall.

Andy was relieved. "Great! So let's get busy. Toby and I have to be back in Hell's Kitchen at five."

Cary grinned at her. "Aren't you forgetting one tiny little detail? Sure, we have the tools. But unless I miss my guess, building a wooden booth without *wood* is not going to be easy!"

Andy's eyes widened. "No wood?" Her eyes scanned the basement's dark depths. "There isn't any wood here?"

Cary shook his head. "We'll have to get it at the lumber yard in the village."

Andy looked as if she might scream at any moment. "But that'll take at least an hour."

"It'll take a lot longer than that. They're not open today. This is Sunday, remember? We'll have to go in tomorrow after classes and get what we need."

"Oh, no!" Her lower lip tightened.

Horrified by the prospect of a girl in tears, Cary grabbed her hand and hustled her back up the stairs and outside. "It'll be okay," he said placatingly as sunlight greeted them. "We'll do other stuff today. Then tomorrow we'll get everything we need. Relax, okay?"

Andy shot him a half-stormy, half-amused look. But as they joined the others and Cary explained the situation, she accepted the fact that they had no choice.

"Okay," Jane said, taking over, "so we can't build booths. But we've got water balloons to fill, cardboard rings to make, posters to paint, and a thousand and one other things to do. So let's quit wasting time and get to it."

They got to it.

But when they had finished, there was no chance to rest. Jane, Toby, and Andy were all due at the Dining Hall to help with the evening meal. Dee and Maggie had ground clean-up outside.

"Wouldn't want to trade me, would you?" Toby asked, hope in her voice. "I'd sure rather be outside than in."

"No way," Dee said with a vigorous shake of her California-blonde hair. "I'm steering clear of kitchen duty. I'll take good old fresh air over frying grease any time."

"Well, you'll have to do it when it's assigned to you," Jane retorted firmly.

"Yeah, well, I can wait until then. Sorry, Toby."

"That's okay. I don't blame you. See y'all later."

Their kitchen chores seemed even worse this time. Some students had skipped breakfast; none seemed willing to skip the evening meal. When the last girl had abandoned her place at the tables, the tired trio was faced with a mountain of dirty dishes, pots and pans, and silverware. The kitchen itself, a large brick-floored room with tile counters, was a mess.

The cooks, two amiable older women, nodded sympathetically. But no offer of help came from either of them.

"Sorry girls," they apologized, donning sweaters and picking up handbags. "But we've got our own families to look after. Good luck!"

The girls were on their own.

Jane's approach didn't make matters better. They had been told to wash the pots and pans by hand as the dishwasher wouldn't get them clean. That job had fallen to Jane, while Andy tackled the mess on the countertops and Toby took on the dining hall tables. Elbow-deep in greasy water, Jane carried on a running tirade against employees who abandon the ship, students who eat too much when a sandwich would do just as well, and the world in general.

"Oh, Jane," Andy finally cried, "knock it off! If you'd quit complaining and concentrate on that scouring pad, you'd get done faster."

Jane whirled in anger. "I don't care! My parents didn't send me to school to learn how to scrub pots and pans!"

Andy slammed her sponge down on the counter and faced her roommate. Her face was damp with perspiration, her yellow shirt smudged and stained. "Well, I don't know where *else* you'd learn how!" she said in exasperation.

That statement stunned Jane for a moment. Then she grinned. "Don't be silly," she said in a lofty voice. "At the Barrett's Boston home, lessons in the proper scrubbing of pots and pans are presented on a regular basis. If one is unable to attend a presentation on one night, one may choose to participate at another time." Then she dipped her arms into the tub of soapsuds and blew a large glob of suds toward Andy.

Laughing, Andy tossed her damp, crumb-covered sponge. It slapped gently against Jane's cheek. Andy grabbed a mop and ran at Jane, jabbing at her roommate's feet. Trailing soapsuds and screeching, Jane took off across the room, taking refuge between the huge white refrigerator and the big old iron stove.

"*What* is going on in here?"

Both girls looked up guiltily, shocked into silence by the sight of their housemother, in jeans and a plaid shirt, standing in the doorway. She was frowning in disapproval.

And where was Toby? Why hadn't she warned them?

"What is going on here?" their housemother repeated, looking around the big kitchen.

"Sorry, Meredith," Jane apologized hastily. She hurried back to the sink. "I guess we got carried away." She attempted a weak smile. "It's been a long day. Sometimes I freak out when I'm really tired."

"Me, too," Andy added, using the mop on the floor where it belonged. "But we're almost done."

"You know, girls," Meredith said sternly, "you don't *have* to do this. Ms. Allardyce is only keeping the school open because you talked her into it. She'll close it in a minute if you want her to."

To Andy's surprise, Jane blurted out, "No! We don't want the school closed! We want to do this!" Then she grinned. "Well, not *this* exactly," gesturing toward the pile of copperbottomed metal. "I could live without this. But we meant what we told P.A. We're willing to do our best. If that means scullery duty, well . . ." she shrugged.

"What's a scullery?" Andy asked innocently, and Jane laughed.

Seeing how tired and disheveled they looked, Meredith took pity on them. "I know how hard you're working," she said. "And I'd help if I could. But I've got my own list of chores, and I've barely made a dent in them."

"Oh, that's okay." Andy scrubbed at a patch of mashed potato on the floor. "We'll be done in no time at all."

Jane wondered, Where have I heard *that* before?

"Good! Well, I'll see you later. Don't forget to lock up. One thing's for sure, all of you will sleep well tonight. Oh, Jane, I almost forgot. I came here specifically to give you a message."

Jane turned around.

"Your mother called."

"Oh?"

"I'm afraid there was a small item in the Boston newspaper about our strike. And your mother apparently found it."

"Oh-oh."

"Exactly. I think you'd better call her back right away."

A campus whose employees were out on strike wouldn't be the sort of place Mrs. Barrett would want her little girl to be.

"I'll call her, Meredith. I'll just finish up here first."

"Okay. See you guys later. If a hot cup of tea sounds more tempting than bed, drop in when you get back to Baker." Meredith smiled. "One of the chores on my list was baking coffee cakes for some very tired girls. I *did* get to that one. Bye."

Compared to facing her mother's reaction

to news of the strike, greasy pots and pans seemed almost a treat. Jane took her time.

When Toby appeared in the doorway, Andy hissed at her, "Where *were* you? Why didn't you warn us Merrie was coming?"

"I'm sorry. I was under the table. I never even saw her until it was too late."

"What on earth were you doing under the table?"

Toby made a face. "Lemon chiffon pie. I think. Although it could have been gravy. Or a blob of butter. Anyway, I'm sorry. Why? What's up?"

"Never mind. She wasn't mad at us, anyway. But it could have been Ms. Allardyce, and then where would we be?"

"On our way home," Jane said grimly. Finishing, she hung the wet dishtowel on a wooden rack over the sink. "Guess what? My mom called. She heard about the strike."

"Oh-oh."

"Exactly."

The three of them stood together in the doorway, surveying the spotless kitchen with satisfaction.

"All that work for nothing," Jane said gloomily. "Because if I know my mother, now that she knows about the strike, she's going to yank me out of here so fast my fingers will still be wrinkled from dishwater."

Walking slowly from a combination of fatigue and depression, the girls locked up and left.

CHAPTER SIX

Taking a deep breath, Jane dialed her home telephone number. The hall was quiet, giving her privacy. People *could* be studying behind all those closed doors. But Jane suspected that most of the girls had probably collapsed, fully clothed, on their beds and fallen asleep. How she wished she were among them!

"Mother? It's Jane. Meredith said you called."

She knew exactly what her mother's reaction to news about the strike would be. "Come home, Jane." And where was she going to get the strength to argue? She was so tired. She felt like a cooked noodle. Every inch of her body had been drained of energy. I *hate* all this work, she thought. But I still don't want to go home. I have to talk her into letting me stay here.

"But I don't want to come home, Mother," she said. "Everything is just fine here, honest!

You can call Ms. Allardyce and ask her if you want. She'll tell you." She'll tell you, Jane thought, because she didn't walk in on the kitchen after dinner tonight, and she didn't see the burned toast this morning, and she wasn't watching my feeble attempts to clean the bathroom.

"Mother. I said everything is fine. We're not starving and yes, of course we've got electricity and plumbing. And of course we're safe. Those weren't guards who walked off the job, they were just maintenance people."

Slumping against the wall, Jane listened to her mother's voice go on and on about her daughter's safety and health and . . .

Maybe now was a good time to follow Andy's example. She had such an honest, open relationship with her parents. Jane had never seen a family who were so close to one another. The Cords seemed to tell each other everything and were so honest about sharing feelings. Barretts, on the other hand, were more likely not to mention feelings. Barretts liked to pretend they didn't *have* feelings. But of course they did have them. They just didn't talk about them. However, desperation called for desperate measures, and she certainly was desperate.

"Mother, please, can I just say something?" Jane's back ached. The absence of a stool in the telephone booth discouraged lengthy phone calls. In another second, she was going to sink straight to the floor because her poor, tired legs were going to give out. "Mother, coming home just now would make me really unhappy. Miserable. I mean it. We're working on the carnival and there's lots to do to get ready, and if I come home I'd just mope around the house thinking about what I could be doing here. Because I'd be feeling really bad."

There. She'd said how she honestly felt. Would it work?

No. Her mother simply said that *she* would feel worse if Jane stayed. So much for discussing feelings.

Okay. Don't give up, Jane, she told herself. Try one more thing.

Standing up very straight in spite of her fatigue, Jane said earnestly, "Mother, I'm sorry, but I just can't afford any time off from classes right now. We're still holding them, you know. It's not the teachers who went on strike. We're nearing the end of the term, and finals. If I come home, I'll never pass those finals. Honest. I won't."

The moment of silence that followed told Jane she'd said exactly the right thing. Relief flooded through her.

There were more questions, of course, but Jane knew she'd won and answered each and every one of them honestly.

"But at the very first hint that things are not going well," Mrs. Barrett finished, sounding very like the headmistress, "you are to phone home immediately, do you understand? And we'll send a car for you right away. Promise me, Jane."

"I promise, Mother. But don't worry, okay? And tell Father I said hello." Her bed was calling to her: Jane . . . come and rest your poor, tired body! She could hear it as clearly as she heard her mother's voice.

But as tired as she was, she didn't go directly to her room after hanging up. She went to the bathroom instead, to brush her teeth, wash her face, just as she always did. Pleased to see that it was still clean, she thought smugly that tomorrow morning, cleaning it would be a piece of cake. Twenty minutes, tops, because she'd done such a super job today. She did hurry through her nightly ritual because she was anxious to share her good news with her roommates. Both girls admired independence and she knew they thought she worried too much about pleasing her parents. She couldn't wait to see the surprise in their faces when she told them she'd won.

She could have taken her time, she realized when she returned to Room 407 and found her roommates, still fully clothed, sprawled across their beds, sound asleep. Toby still had her cowboy boots on.

"I'll bet," Jane said softly to herself as she covered each girl with a blanket, "I could yank both of them onto the floor, and they wouldn't move a muscle." Then, giggling softly to herself at such a picture, she crawled into her own bed and gave in to her fatigue.

At least seventy-five percent of the weary Canby Hall student body overslept on Monday. Those who hadn't were given the unpleasant task of rousing the ones who had. Toby, always an early riser, awoke at her usual time. Resisting the temptation to let her roommates sleep off their weariness, she woke them. It wasn't easy.

"Andy, we're going to be late!"

No answer. No movement. Andy could just as easily have been a store mannequin.

"Jane, get up. You have the bathroom to do again, remember?"

Jane opened one eye. Realizing that one eye open just wasn't enough, Toby grabbed Jane's foot and shook it. "Bathroom? Remember?"

"I want to die," Jane said softly. "I don't want to go near that stupid bathroom. I don't want to move one muscle off this bed. Go away and leave me alone." But she sat up, shaking her head sadly. "Why," she asked Toby in a mournful voice, "why are the girls in this school such slobs? You wouldn't believe that bathroom yesterday. I should have just put a "Condemned" sign on it and locked it up."

Toby continued to shake Andy, who was beginning to mutter in protest.

"Well," Jane said in a more optimistic tone,

"at least it won't take me so long this morning. I just super-cleaned the whole thing yesterday." She got out of bed, wincing as any number of muscles shrieked in agony. "I can't wait for you guys, though. If I don't go grab something to eat right now, I won't have time to hit the bathroom before class." She changed into a sweatsuit and was gone before Andy was fully awake.

In spite of her aches and pains, Jane did feel optimistic as she hurried across campus. The late spring air felt fresh and clean, she wasn't going to be yanked off campus after all, and Cary wasn't around to get a look at her in this horrid sweatsuit. She'd change out of it before classes. She'd get something in her stomach, make short work of the bathroom, and get to class. And this afternoon the guys would go get the lumber so they could start work on the booths. Things could be a lot worse.

She was further cheered by the calm in an almost-empty Dining Hall. She gulped down her cereal and hurried out of the Dining Hall, hoping the late-risers had all skipped their morning showers and were done in the bathroom.

Moments later, she stood in shock just inside the bathroom door. Someone had stolen her nice, clean bathroom. They had replaced it with a conglomeration of wet towels, toothpaste smears and soap smudges, dirty laundry, crumpled paper towels, and wet puddles on the floor. The same floor she'd diligently mopped just yesterday. Twenty-four short hours ago. *One* day. How could anyone make this much mess in just one day?

"I don't *believe* this!" Jane moaned, the pail on her arm sagging as she sagged. Two things struck her then: that girls in a hurry were even worse than girls not in a hurry, and that the cleaning staff did this stuff EVERY SINGLE DAY. They did it on Monday and then they did it again on Tuesday and then they did it again on Wednesday. How awful. How truly awful, to spend your whole life picking up somebody else's wet towels. Why would someone do that?

A little voice inside her said, Could it have something to do with money — and survival.

Guilt overcame her anger. Just knowing she would never, ever have to do this every day for a living made her feel both lucky and ashamed. And when all of this was over, maybe she'd be more careful about where she threw her dirty towels and laundry.

Still, couldn't they have waited until she graduated to go on strike? Allowing herself one more hearty groan, Jane went to work.

Very few girls made it to their first class on time. No one from Room 407 did, thanks to latecomers straggling into the Dining Hall. But sympathetic teachers, who didn't want the school closed any more than the students did, marked no one tardy. And not one teacher assigned homework.

Not that the girls would have had time to do it. Jane, who had done much of the organizing of the chore charts, couldn't understand why they were so swamped with work.

"There are enough girls in this school," she said at lunch, "to get things done. What are we doing wrong?" She glanced around the table. Her lunch sat in front of her, untouched. She was too tired to eat.

"Haven't you heard?" Maggie asked. "A lot of parents read about the strike. At least thirty girls have already gone home, and a bunch are leaving tomorrow. So the chore charts have been all messed up."

"Oh, no!" Jane couldn't believe it. "After all the work we did on them!" Angry tears sparkled in her blue eyes. "It was all a waste of time. How can we possibly manage with fewer girls?"

"We can," Andy said calmly but firmly. "We'll just go over the charts and eliminate the girls who've gone. Dee, you get a list of the girls who left. Try P.A.'s secretary."

"Gosh, Andy," Toby pointed out, "that's going to mean more work for everybody. I don't know . . ."

"Oh, I *hate* this stupid strike!" Jane cried, angrily jamming her straw into her little milk carton. "Everything is getting so messed up." It was impossible to believe she'd felt so good earlier that same day.

"Don't blame the strikers," Andy cautioned. "Why couldn't the parents have left their little darlings right here where they could help? They could learn something, too. I can't believe how many girls at this school don't knew the first thing about housework."

Chaotic bathroom scenes floated before Jane's eyes. She nodded grimly.

Andy continued heatedly, "I sure would hate to share an apartment with any of the girls who sat at the middle table at breakfast this morning. Yuk! Talk about slobs. . . ."

It was Toby's turn to nod. "When they left, their table looked like a garbage can attacked by a family of raccoons."

Dee arrived just then. "Maybe," she said thoughtfully as she plunked her tray down, "maybe we should make a new rule. We could call it an emergency rule."

Everyone looked up at her with interest.

She sat down. "Why shouldn't each girl clean up her own mess in the Dining Hall? Take her tray into the kitchen, rinse off her dishes, put them in the dishwasher, and throw out her own trash?"

Jane grinned. "That," she said emphatically, "is not a bad idea. In fact, it's a great idea. That would free up the kitchen help. They'd get done with the other stuff faster."

"Besides," Toby added, "why shouldn't each girl carry her own load? It'll be educational, right?" No one waited on the guys in the bunkhouse at home. Cookie just cooked, he didn't pick up after the hands. They did that themselves.

Unanimously agreeing, they approached the two cooks. One was for it. One was not. Patting Dee on the shoulder, she said, "I know you mean well, child. But, my goodness, we can't have all those girls traipsing in and out of here. Why, we'd all be falling all over ourselves."

But she gave in when they convinced her that they'd make sure the girls were orderly. "They can all come into just this one area," Andy promised, standing in front of the dishwasher. "And they'll just zip in and zip right back out, quickly. Please. It would help a lot, I think."

"Well, all right," the cook said. "But if I find too many girls underfoot, we'll have to go back to the old way."

"Right," Andy said with a happy smile. They left the dining hall congratulating themselves.

"It's not a lot," Jane said, "but every little bit helps. Now! Let's make short work of our afternoon classes so we can move on to carnival work before dinner. Geniuses that we are, class should be no problem at all."

Her companions grinned. "No problem at all!"

Laughing, they hurried across campus.

CHAPTER SEVEN

At three-fifteen, the girls from Room 407 were just coming out of Baker House, when Randy Crowell's old pickup truck came up the tree-lined driveway and parked. Randy jumped to the ground, calling out a friendly "Hi!" Sunburned, tall and lanky, in old jeans and a Greenleaf Dragons high school T-shirt, he looked every inch the healthy farm man, which was exactly what he was. Toby smiled. Although she was giving up on the idea of Randy ever being her boyfriend, she still thought of him as a friend and was always glad to see him. He understood how restless she got when the long New England winter tried to keep her cooped up inside like a bird in a cage. It was that very restlessness that had led her, last fall, over the hill behind Baker, where she'd discovered the Crowell farm. Randy was five years older that she was and persisted in treating her like a younger sister or cousin. Now that she dated Neal Worthington, that didn't sting as much as it once had. And she could go riding at the Crowell place any time she wanted.

"Heard there was some trouble over here," Randy said. He always got right to the point. "Thought maybe I could help."

"That's real nice of you," Toby said, just as two cars full of Oakley Prep boys arrived. "And I'll bet you can help. These boys have to go into the village to get lumber for our carnival booths. The wood we need isn't going to fit into those little-bitty cars. Could we maybe borrow your truck?"

"Sure. You bet. I'll even drive you all there myself."

"Great idea," Cary approved, joining them. Jane sighed, seeing his paint-stained cut-offs and grimy T-shirt, but said nothing. He *was* going to be working, after all. "If we have the wood delivered, it won't get here until tomorrow. That would mean another wasted day. Thanks, Crowell."

"My pleasure. Ready to go?"

"Who's going with Randy?" Cary wanted to know, turning to the group.

Everyone wanted to go, but Jane put her foot down. "We all can't go. There isn't room in the truck for all that lumber and all of us. Besides, it'll save time if some of us stay here and collect tools, nails, and stuff like that. We can have everything set up when the lumber arrives."

"Toby," Randy said pleasantly, "how about if you come along? You can be the official representative from Canby Hall." He smiled as he said it. Jane thought to herself, Neal would be a little jealous if he saw how great these two look together. Maybe a lot jealous.

"Here," she said, handing Toby a piece of paper. "It's Meredith's authorization for charging the lumber. Mr. Lombardi at the lumberyard will ask for it."

As Toby and Randy climbed into the truck's cab, Matt and two of Cary's friends from Ambulance climbed in the back. They would, they said, help load the lumber and see that it didn't take off during the bumpy ride home.

When the truck had pulled away, Andy announced, "I'll help you guys in a few minutes. But first I'm going to collect some cold drinks at the Dining Hall and take them to those people on the picket line." She glanced up at the sun. "It's hot out here. Those poor people must be as dry as Toby's Texas."

Jane stared at her. "Those poor people," she said angrily, "are why we're going through all of this. You're not *really* going to baby them, are you?"

"Yes," Andy said, "I really *are*. Jane, why can't you just put yourself in their shoes?"

"She can't do that," Cary said, deadpan, "because not one of them is wearing hand-crafted leather Italian shoes."

"Cary! That's not funny!" Jane said.

Cary didn't apologize. Andy added hastily, "Jane, you know how hard we've been working, just for a couple of days. Those people on the picket line do it all the time. *All* the time!"

Since Jane had had identical thoughts while cleaning the bathroom that morning, she was at a loss for words.

"Maggie? Dee? Want to help me?" The two girls nodded. "Jane," Andy said, "you and Cary can collect the tools. We won't be gone long."

Jane and Cary watched them go. "Andy's a good kid," he said as they disappeared from view. "She understands how hard this is for those people over there."

Jane faced him, angry red spots high on her cheeks. "Oh, and I don't, I suppose."

"I don't expect you to. I just wish you'd try, that's all."

Why did everyone seem to think she wasn't trying. She held out reddened hands. Two of the fingernails were broken and although it was killing her to see them like that, she just hadn't had time to file them. "Does *that* look like I'm not trying?" she demanded.

Laughing sympathetically, Cary said, "Poor Jane," and slipped an arm around her shoulders. They began walking toward Baker House and its basement tools. "Everyone wants you to be someone you're not. Still," he added calmly, "if you're going to be a writer, you'll have to start imagining how other people think and feel. People just like those strikers over there, for instance."

"When I start telling you how to play your music," she said, sending out syllables splintered in ice, "you can tell me how to be a writer."

"Well, excuse *me*," he said mildly. "If you don't mind people thinking you're a snob with that attitude of yours about the strike, so be it. I won't say another word."

Jane clenched her teeth. I'm not a snob, I'm not a snob, I am not a snob!

A cold silence enveloped them as they collected the necessary tools.

The striking workers were grateful to Andy, Dee, and Maggie for the cold drinks they'd begged from the two cooks, who were also eager to help their fellow workers. One of them had dumped a huge pile of freshly baked chocolate chip cookies into the cardboard carton full of drinks Andy was carrying.

A short, heavy-set man in white T-shirt and jeans accepted a drink gratefully. "Sorry for all the trouble we're causing you girls," he said after a long, thirsty swallow. "Can't be helped, y'know."

Andy shrugged. "That's okay. We're managing. Have any of you talked to anyone on the Board of Trustees?"

A woman in a gray dress that matched her hair said, "Hmph! Fat chance! They won't see us."

Andy frowned. "How can the strike get settled if you aren't talking to each other?"

A young man Andy had seen clipping hedges the week before, took a cookie. "They figure if they freeze us out, we'll give up." He had a lot of brown hair, and he shook it vigorously. "But we won't! We're not giving up until we get our hours back. Right?" he shouted.

"Right!" the crowd agreed.

A man Andy knew as Leo, a carpenter who had built some shelves in their bathroom, called to her. "You kids finding everything you need for your carnival?"

"So far," she said. "The booths are going to be our biggest problem. Some of the guys from Oakley just went to pick up the lumber." She laughed. "You'll have to check the booths out when we're done. Most of us don't know a hammer from a hole in the ground."

"Listen," he said, lowering his voice, "you have any problems, you come to me, you hear? Been making them booths for seven years now. Could do it in my sleep, had I a mind to."

"Oh, thanks, Leo! That's really nice of you."

"Well, it's a nice thing you're doin' here. 'Preciate it."

When the three girls returned to the spot on campus where Cary and Jane were laying out the tools, Andy told them about Leo's offer of help. Cary grinned, but Jane silently continued to arrange nails in neat little piles.

Andy shrugged. She didn't feel like arguing with Jane. Arguing would ruin her good mood. The people on the picket line had been so nice, so grateful. Maybe they could do the same thing tomorrow for the strikers. Why not?

She wished the guys and Toby would hurry up. Now that she knew where to go for help if they needed it, she was anxious to get going on the booths and the dunk tank. Where *were* they, anyway? What was taking so long?

What was taking so long was a large pizza. With mushrooms. And extra cheese. No anchovies. Toby had argued against it, saying nervously that everyone was waiting for them back at school. But she'd been outvoted by four boys who hadn't had a pizza in over twenty-four hours. "Besides," Matt had said calmly, "we have to wait for all that lumber. Mr. Lombardi said it would take about half an hour to get it ready. That's plenty of time for a pizza."

But Pizza Pete's was crowded and they had to wait for a table. Then they had to wait for the pizza. The minutes whizzed by. Toby was shocked when she saw what time it was.

Toby wasn't used to, and didn't like, the feeling of being irresponsible. They had promised to do something; they had promised to hurry, and that wasn't what they were doing.

"C'mon, you guys," she urged, "eat up!"

Just when she'd decided nobody in the whole world chewed as slowly as Matt did, Randy pushed back his chair and said, "Toby's right. We've been here too long. C'mon, let's go."

On the way back to the lumberyard, Toby tried to tell herself they might still have time to work on the booths today. But it was no use. They would be due at the Dining Hall soon. The boys had offered to stay and work through their own dinner hour (thanks to the pizza), but it would be dark soon, which gave them very little time to work. Hammering booths together in the darkness would be downright dangerous. All they would probably have time to do was unload the truck. Everything else would have to wait until tomorrow.

Loading the truck took less time than she'd feared. All four boys helped. Toby went into the office to give Mr. Lombardi the voucher from Meredith.

He looked at it silently for a moment. Then he shook his balding head. "Sorry, miss," he said, "but I can't take this. I need cash. No cash, no lumber." And while a stupefied Toby stood by silently, the big man yelled through the open door, "Hey, hold up on that truck! We got a problem here."

CHAPTER EIGHT

Toby stood inside the little office that smelled of sawdust, staring open-mouthed at the big man in blue overalls.

"Excuse me?" she asked politely.

"I said, this voucher isn't any good to me."

"Well, I know that's what you said. But I don't understand. Meredith Pembroke, our housemother, said Canby always pays with vouchers. Then the school pays all the bills at the end of the month."

Mr. Lombardi hooked his thumbs around the straps of his overalls. "That's the way it was before the strike, miss. But with all that stuff going on up at the school and nobody knowing what's going to happen, I have to have cash. Sorry."

Toby thought, He thinks the school's going to close and he won't get his money. "I don't *have* any cash, Mr. Lombardi," she said softly. "And by the time we went all the way back to school to get it and came back here, the lumberyard would be closed for the day."

He nodded. "Yep, prob'ly so."

Randy thudded up the steps and came inside. "What's the hold-up?"

"Hold-up is right," Toby murmured. "He says he has to have cash."

Scowling, Randy turned to the owner. "What? Oh, come on, Pete. You know the students don't carry that kind of cash around with them. Take the voucher and let us leave."

"Now, wait just a minute, Crowell. . . ."

"No, *you* wait a minute. We do a lot of business with you, Lombardi, and so does the school. You owe them some kind of loyalty now, don't you think?"

Toby didn't want Randy fighting Canby Hall's battles. He wasn't even a student there.

"Mr. Lombardi," she said, stepping forward, "if I call the school and get our headmistress's guarantee that you'll receive your money, will you let us take the lumber?"

The man hesitated. But the girl was so determined. And Canby Hall had always paid its bills in the past. Maybe he was making too much of the strike. After all, the school hadn't closed, had it?

"Oh, all right," he said, "go ahead and take the lumber." He grinned at Toby. "I don't get my money, I'll just come out there and have you all arrested."

Toby forced a weak laugh. "Right! You know where to find us." She turned then and, tugging at Randy's sleeve, left the office, calling cheerfully over her shoulder, "See you in jail!"

In the truck, she breathed a huge sigh of relief. As Randy started the truck, she confided, "I'm so glad I didn't have to call P.A. I don't have the slightest notion what I'd have said to her."

"You did okay in there," Randy said admiringly. "Really stuck up for yourself."

"Thanks. I was as nervous as a piece of cheese in a mouse trap, for a while there. Jane and Andy are going to be mad enough that we're getting back so late. If we came back with an empty truck, they'd probably have steam coming out of their ears."

It would serve her right if Jane never spoke to her again.

Jane wasn't quite ready to stop speaking to Toby. Not just yet. She managed to slip a few well-chosen words from between lips tight with anger. "We have been sitting here waiting for you for*ever*! The whole day is wasted. Where have you guys *been?*"

"We ran into some trouble about the voucher," Toby murmured guiltily, knowing that wasn't exactly the whole truth. The boys began unloading the lumber, stacking it in neat piles on the lawn.

"Oh, yeah?" Jane's eyes narrowed as they focused on a large orange spot on Toby's long-sleeved white sweater. "Where? At Pizza Pete's?"

Toby flushed. She felt the eyes of everyone in the group accusing her.

"Look, everyone," Cary said, coming to her rescue, "it's no big deal. So they stopped for pizza. So what? They had to wait for the lumber, anyway."

Jane turned a scornful gaze on him. "I should have known you'd defend them. That's just the kind of thing *you'd* do, going for pizza when people are counting on you."

Cary held his hands up in front of him. "Whoa! We don't have time to fight." Shaking his head, he walked away, joining the boys at the truck.

"Now look what you've done!" Jane hissed at Toby. "Cary's mad at me and it's all your fault."

Toby was perfectly willing to take responsibility for being so late. But not for Jane's personal problems. "When it comes to making Cary ornery," she drawled, "I don't think you need help from me or anyone else." Turning to the others, she said, "Jane's right about one thing, though. We had no business fooling around at Pizza Pete's. I'm really sorry."

"What happened with the voucher?" Andy wanted to know. She wanted to know, but more than that, she wanted the subject changed. The afternoon was gone, so what was the point of arguing? They could start work on the booths tomorrow.

They all listened as Toby explained what had happened. Jane's relief that the voucher had been accepted eased her anger somewhat. The last of it disappeared when Randy called out, "Yeah, you should have seen Toby. She was great! Lombardi was no match for her."

Jane's perfectly tweezed eyebrows arched. "Well, good for you, Toby! If you'd backed down, we would have lost another whole day of work." Jane really didn't like being angry. It seemed, somehow, uncivilized. Probably, she thought generously, I'd have gone for pizza, too.

Two seconds later, she said briskly, "Okay, so we'll all meet here tomorrow after classes, right?" Then, she added hastily, "If that's okay with everyone."

It was. The trio from Room 407 hurried off to the Dining Hall. Maggie and Dee and the other girls returned to Baker House to do their chores, and the Oakley Prep group and Randy Crowell went home. The piles of lumber stayed where they were, patiently waiting for hammer and nail.

Because of the new rules about each girl clearing up her own mess, dining hall chores that night were a bit lighter. But it was all still too time-consuming to suit Andy.

"Ms. Lafferty," she asked one of the cooks as the women prepared to leave, "why couldn't we have simpler meals, just for a while? Things like soup and sandwiches and salad. It would be a lot easier to clean up after meals and," she added cleverly, "it would make your job easier, too."

Ms. Lafferty, who was plump, gray-haired, and rosy-cheeked from the heat of the oven, looked interested for a moment. Then she shook her head. "Growing girls need hearty foods," she said firmly, "things that stick to your ribs."

Andy looked down with distaste at the food-encrusted kettle in her hands. "Not to mention the cookware," she muttered under her breath. Aloud, she said, "Things like mashed potatoes, you mean?" being careful not to use descriptive words such as gluey or gummy.

The woman nodded and picked up her purse. "That's right, dear," and then added an expression Andy was sure she'd picked up from a television talk show, "We are what we eat, you know."

Andy shuddered. "But Ms. Lafferty," she argued gently, "being an expert on nutrition, you must know vegetables are just the best thing in the world for growing girls. And most of us *like* salad and vegetable soup."

Ms. Grissom, the second cook, came to her aid. "She's right, Edna. I was saying myself, just the other day, these girls don't eat near enough fresh vegetables. And sandwiches, well, my goodness, my Archie's been carrying sandwiches in his lunch pail every day for forty years, and he's as healthy as a horse."

Andy sensed that both women were tempted by the idea of simpler meals. Such a change would send them home earlier to their own families every night.

She went in for the kill. Sighing heavily, she said, "It must take just hours to fix all that roast beef and potatoes and chicken and meat loaf all the time."

Heaving an identical sigh, Ms. Lafferty nodded. "That it does, child, that it does." She looked at Ms. Grissom for support or argument. Ms. Grissom simply shrugged.

"All right," Ms. Lafferty said, "but the missus will have to give her okay." The "missus" was Ms. Allardyce. "You girls, you make up some new menus with the stuff you just talked about, salads and the like, and take them to her. If she gives the okay, me and Rose here will go along."

Andy breathed a huge sigh of relief. A delighted grin creased her face, quickly matched by those of Jane and Toby, who had heard the entire conversation.

After warning Andy once more that Ms. Allardyce would have to initial the new, easier menus, the two women left.

The three girls jumped up and down, shouting with glee. "All *right!*" Andy cried, banging on her kettle with a wooden spoon and marching around the kitchen. "No more green, gluey stuff! No more gray blobs of whatsis! No more unidentifiable frying objects!"

"Whoa, wait a sec!" Toby cautioned. "We don't have P.A.'s okay yet. She might not go for it."

"Yeah," Jane agreed, looking doubtful.

"Are we willing to face her again? So soon? She's going to get sick of us."

That thought sobered all of them. Then Andy grinned. "I know what," she said, "let's ask Merrie. She's a vegetarian. I know she'll like our idea. We'll ask *her* to take it to P.A."

"Think she'll do it?" Toby asked as she returned to her floor-mopping.

"It can't hurt to ask. Hey, do you realize that we're making all these changes in the kitchen, and we won't even be here tomorrow. Three girls from Addison are scheduled."

"Don't worry, Andy," Jane pointed out, wiping the tile counters with a sponge, "unless the strike is settled pretty soon, we'll be back here."

"True. Sad, but true."

When they returned to Baker House, they went straight upstairs to Meredith's apartment. She was enthusiastic about their idea and offered to create the sort of menus they had in mind. "I'll take them to Ms. Allardyce as soon as I have enough for several days," she told them. Relieved, they thanked her and left.

"I *knew* Merrie was okay," Andy babbled happily on their way back down the stairs. "Isn't she terrific? It could have taken hours for us to do those menus. Now we don't have to and we can rest. Gee, isn't everything working out well?"

Well, not quite everything, they discovered as they reached the fourth floor. It quickly became painfully obvious that Baker House wasn't faring well during the strike. Unmade beds shouted at them from every open door. The door to the fourth-floor broom closet also stood open, revealing a jumble of cleaning tools carelessly tossed inside, several plastic pails still filled with dirty soapsuds, and more than one pile of dusting cloths cluttering up the tile floor.

"Oh, no!" Jane cried. "Did we miss the earthquake?"

"What a mess!" Andy agreed, stepping into the closet. "Who *did* this?"

"Are you kidding?" Jane asked, leaning wearily against the doorway. "Our little Baker House homemakers, that's who!" She groaned. "I am not stepping one foot inside that bathroom tonight, I don't care if my face falls off! If they could do this to a mere broom closet, think what they could do to my nice, clean bathroom!"

Andy emptied the pails into the old metal sink and hung them on the wall. Toby gathered the rags together and enclosed them in a large plastic bag.

"That's enough," Jane ordered. "We are not supposed to be doing this. We've done our part today."

"I know," Toby agreed, "but if Ms. Allardyce saw this . . ."

"Toby. Ms. Allardyce doesn't run around haunting the halls at night. She's probably safe at home, so quit worrying, okay?"

Nodding doubtfully, Toby left the closet, with Andy close on her heels. But just to be on the safe side, they closed the door firmly behind them.

Maggie was standing by the door of 407. "Toby!" she called, "hurry up! Telephone. It's long-distance. I heard your phone and went in to answer it."

Toby's green eyes lit up. It wouldn't be her father. He didn't believe in long-distance calls except in cases of dire emergency. That only left one person: Cornelius Worthington III. Great! Smiling, she hurried into her room to the telephone.

Watching her, Andy felt a sharp pang of regret for the movie date with Matt she'd had to cancel. There wouldn't be any movies for a while. Who had time? Oh, well, she told herself, Toby's Neal was in Boston. At least Matt was here and would be helping with the carnival.

True to her word, Jane avoided the bathroom, going straight to her bed. Andy followed suit.

It was just as well, since, as they both learned the first thing the following morning, there wasn't a single clean towel in all of Baker Hall. Not knowing that until morning would give them a decent night's sleep.

CHAPTER NINE

"Hi, Toby," Neal said when she said hello. His voice over the telephone was warm and strong. "I just wondered how you were holding up. My parents told me about the strike. They heard it from Jane's folks."

"I'm okay," Toby said softly. "It's kind of hectic, that's all. Did your mom tell you what we're doing? How we're keeping the school open?"

Neal laughed. She could picture him as clearly as if he were standing right there beside her: tall, blond, with kind blue eyes. She'd been drawn to those eyes the first time she saw him. But she'd thought he was Jane's boyfriend. She had also thought the chances of someone like Neal being interested in a long-legged hick from the sticks were about as good as the chances of snowflakes in Texas in July. She still couldn't believe she'd been wrong about that.

"She sure did. Somehow, I can't see Jane doing housework."

"Oh, Jane can do anything," Toby said loyally.

"Yeah, I guess. But washing dishes? Mopping a floor? Somehow my brain has trouble with that image. It reminds me of those puzzles when we were kids, remember? Those 'what's wrong with this picture' puzzles."

Toby hadn't spent a lot of time doing puzzles as a child. That was an indoor activity. And she didn't want to talk about Jane. "It's the same with a lot of kids here," she said. "They don't know much about housework. We promised Ms. Allardyce we'd do what the strikers did, but we forgot to ask first if everyone knew what a vacuum cleaner is."

Neal laughed again. "Ah, the privileged upper-classes," he said knowingly. "We don't get a lot of lessons in such mundane things as cleaning a bathroom, Toby. Our parents like to believe we'll never need that stuff."

"Well, we need it now," she said grimly. "Trouble is, we don't have it. If Ms. A. pays us a surprise visit to check out how we're doing, first she'll go into cardiac arrest, and then the school will be closed."

Neal was silent for a moment before saying softly, "I don't want you to go back to Texas. It's too far away. I wish you were here right now."

"Oh, so do I." And she thought, Boy, do I!

To be away from all of this, to be with Neal, wouldn't that be nice? If only . . .

"Look, is there anything I can do?"

Toby laughed. "Just do what you're doing now. Call to cheer me up every once in a while."

"My pleasure. You take care of yourself, okay? And I'm still planning on coming for that carnival of yours. It's still on, right?"

Toby pictured the pile of lumber sitting on the lawn, a bunch of boards not good for much of anything at the moment. "It's still on," she said. "But it might be a really good idea for you to check first before you come on up here. We're not that sure we're going to get things pulled together in time."

"Okay. Will do. Take care now, okay?"

That sounded nice. "You, too," she said, meaning it.

She hung up the phone with a dreamy smile on her face.

Which was erased as she realized Jane and Andy had only been waiting for her to get off the phone to become embroiled in another heated discussion about the strike.

"*Look* at this!" Jane cried, thrusting something that was colored a horrid shade of pea-green under Toby's nose. "This," she said with disgust, "was one of my Wedgwood blue sheets. Notice I said 'was.' Thanks to that totally stupid Miller Beaumont, it is now the color of a soup I positively loathe! How can anyone expect me to *sleep* on this?"

"Jane," Andy said coolly, "you'll be asleep. You won't even know that your sheets are clashing with your precious Wedgwood blue walls."

"What happened?" Toby asked, moving quickly between Andy and Jane to intercept the daggers being sent Andy's way. "To the sheet, I mean?"

Jane shook her head. "Miller decided to toss one of her blouses in with the sheets. Can you believe it? And the color ran, of course. *All over my sheets!*"

"Don't get so excited," Andy said, wrapping her arms around an old teddy bear.

"If it weren't for this stupid strike," Jane retorted angrily, "Miller Beaumont would never have laid her hands on my sheets. She would have continued to use those lily-white hands of hers for nothing more important than painting her nails. And she would have *left my sheets alone!*"

"Look who's talking," Andy said harshly. "The very person who collected all the dirty towels in the bathroom and then dumped them in the laundry room on the floor, as if they would magically jump into the washing machine all by themselves."

"No one told me I was supposed to wash those towels."

"Jane, we talked about it when we made up the charts. We decided that washing the towels should be done by the person who cleaned the bathroom."

"I forgot. Anyway, that's just too much work for one person. I agreed to that before I found out just how much work was involved in cleaning one bathroom. From now on, we'll assign someone who isn't doing anything else to do the laundry."

"There isn't anyone who isn't doing anything else. Everyone is overloaded as it is."

Jane jumped on that remark. "See? Isn't that what I was just saying? Because of this stupid strike, which isn't going to get anybody anywhere, we're all tired and cranky."

"Well, *you* certainly are! And who says the strike isn't going to do any good? How do you know that? You don't know the first thing about labor."

"Oh, I give up! This is ridiculous. I'm going to bed."

"Good. And don't talk in your sleep."

The two of them fell silent then. Toby sighed in relief. At least she had Neal's phone call to comfort her. She would hang onto that.

Clean or not, Baker House fell silent as well, as its weary occupants welcomed sleep.

And they awoke the next morning to a light but steady rain tapping against the windows.

Toby awoke first. Oh, no! Not rain. Not today. Any other time she would have welcomed it. She wasn't used to frequent rain, and it delighted her. But that lumber was sitting out there, waiting for them. How could they work in the rain? Would it stop by this afternoon? Would the wood be too wet to use? Depressing, depressing, depressing!

Then she remembered. Today was her day to work outside, watering the tulip beds. She grinned. Mother Nature was letting her off the hook. What did that mean? Did she then have the day off? No chores? Shaking her head, Toby told herself a day off wasn't likely. There was just too much to do.

"I don't believe this!" Jane cried when she woke up and realized it was raining.

"*Now* what are we going to do?" Andy wanted to know rubbing her eyes.

"Well, there's plenty of stuff to do inside," Toby pointed out gently.

"That won't help the carnival," Jane said. "I hate to say this, but if we don't start making some real progress pretty soon, we might have to cancel the whole thing."

Her roommates stared at her.

"No," Andy said firmly, "no way. Jane, we've already hung posters and printed up tickets. And we bought all that lumber."

"Yeah. A lot of good that's going to do us today." Jane went to the window and stood there, looking out on the gloomy spring day.

"We won't have to cancel it," Andy said reassuringly. "First of all, this rain isn't going to last all day. I promise. And second," as she pulled a red sweater over her head, "not a single girl is scheduled to be taken out of school today. So we won't have to redo the charts again. That's a good sign, right?"

Allowing herself to be cheered a little by Andy's optimism, Jane reached for the chore charts. "Okay, who's got what today? Addison has dining hall, and Connie and Joan have our bathroom, and Andy, you can do the laundry. I'll take the hall. Toby?"

Toby grinned. "I," she announced with a certain amount of smugness, "am scheduled for outside watering."

"That's not fair! Why couldn't I have that? Then I'd have a whole day off until time to work on the carnival."

Toby and Andy laughed. "Oh, Jane," Toby said between giggles, "you gave *me* that job because you couldn't see yourself grubbing around in a bed of dirt. I'm trying to picture it now and I'm having trouble."

"Does not compute," Andy said in a robot-like voice.

"Okay, okay." But Jane wasn't about to let Toby off the hook completely. "You can vacuum the lobby downstairs. Toni Dodd was supposed to do it, but she's already gone home."

Toby shrugged. "Okay. I can handle that. I'd feel funny sitting around while everyone else is working, anyway."

The girls of Canby Hall watched the sky all day. In class, the girls closest to the windows passed clues to the others: If eyes were rolled in despair, it was still raining. If the sky looked like it might clear, smiles of hope were turned to the rest of the class.

When the last bell rang and the students poured out onto the lawn, they were greeted by a pale sun peeking down from behind the last of the clouds. A jubilant cheer filled the air — they could get some work done on the carnival, after all.

"Hey, wait a sec!" Jane called, calming everyone down. "That lumber is going to be soaked." She frowned. "Anybody know if you can build stuff out of wet wood?"

No one did. Jane stepped around one of the puddles decorating the lawn. "Well, let's all go change our clothes and meet at the lumber pile. We'll deal with it then."

But when they got there, the wood wasn't wet. It was completely covered with several heavy black tarpaulins. The wood was snug and dry.

Everyone looked at Andy. "When did you do this?" Jane asked, her eyes wide.

"I didn't do it. I never even thought of it. Besides, I wouldn't have known where the tarps are kept." They were all still trying to figure out who had protected their lumber from the rain when the boys arrived. They denied knowing anything about the tarps. "But let's get to work," Cary said, "in case it decides to rain again."

Armed with the booth plans in Andy's fat black notebook, the crowd began sawing and hammering, warmed now by a full-strength sun.

They were all working away steadily when

Andy suddenly cried, "I know! I know who covered the wood. It had to be Leo."

"Leo?" Cary echoed.

"The carpenter, the one who's been making the booths for years. I talked to him on the picket line. He would know where the tarps are kept."

Jane threw her an annoyed look.

"No, listen, he was really nice yesterday and he said if we needed any help with the booths, to let him know. He would have passed the lumber on his way to the picket line this morning. I'm sure it was him."

"Must be a neat guy," Matt said, hoisting a thick sheet of wood off the pile and onto the tarps.

"There are a lot of nice people on the picket line," Andy said, returning Jane's glare. "And that reminds me. They've been out in the rain all day. Anybody want to help me take coffee over there? I'm sure they could use it."

Dee and Maggie volunteered in spite of Jane's impatient, "Oh, Andy, come on! We've got work to do here."

"We won't be gone that long. Besides, you've got plenty of help here. There aren't even enough hammers to go around."

That was true enough. When it became clear that only a certain number of hands was necessary to get the job done, many of the girls left to attend to their indoor chores. Those who remained behind quickly discovered that putting pieces of wood together wasn't as easy as it sounded. The most frequently uttered word that afternoon was "Ouch!" as hammer missed nail and landed instead on a thumb or finger.

Jane, in particular, found herself out of her depth.

"Hey, Jane," Cary said, wiping sweat from his brow, "how about taking a couple of people and going for cold drinks?"

It was humiliating. Cary was pointing out to everyone that she was only good for fetching and carrying. The worst part was, at this particular point in time, he was right.

He put one hand on her shoulder, and she shook it away. "Okay," she said crisply, "I can do that. Leslie? David? C'mon, let's go get cold drinks for everyone. If Andy can take coffee to the strikers, I guess we can do the same for our workers here."

Her mother had told her more than once, "Jane, whatever you do, do it with dignity." So, although running this little errand seemed beneath her, she walked ahead of the other two with her head high, her back straight. And during the walk to the Dining Hall, she uttered not one word of complaint about the strike, even though the truth was, she was beginning to hate it with a ferocity that surprised even her.

Because it was ruining everything. Everything.

CHAPTER TEN

Jane was still fuming when she ran into
Meredith. In jeans and a yellow sweatshirt,
Merrie was making her way across campus, a
piece of white paper in her hands.

"Okay, here's the deal," she said as she
reached Jane. "Ms. Allardyce has okayed the
menus. But the cooks tell me they'll need supplies from town. I have to go into the village
to pick up office supplies for the teachers. If
I give you the grocery list, could you run into
the market and get what's needed in the
kitchen? I'll give you cash so you won't run
into any problems with the voucher, okay?"

Jane hesitated. Everyone was waiting for
cold drinks. But this was a chance to get away
from it all and go into the village. Besides,
Cary had no business treating her like a
waitress. "Sure! I can't wait to see everyone's
face tonight in the Dining Hall when they
aren't served green sludge. Just let me run

up and throw something decent on, and get my purse."

"Okay, but make it snappy. It's getting late and there's quite a bit to get. Mostly fresh fruits and veggies, and sandwich makings. You'll have to have it delivered, it's too much to carry or to fit into my car." She frowned. "You probably haven't had much experience shopping for food, have you, Jane?"

The doubt in Meredith's voice annoyed Jane. Didn't anybody think she could do *any-thing*? "No problem," she said. "After all, I've been *eating* for years. That should have taught me something about food. If I can eat it, I can certainly buy it."

But not *here*, she decided after a short ten minutes in the village supermarket. The quality of food was, it seemed to Jane, absolutely disgraceful. Her list included bread, sandwich fillings and condiments, and the fresh fruit and vegetables Meredith had mentioned. The bread felt to her touch like wet sponges, the cold cuts in the delicatessen section seemed to her critical eye to have a greenish tinge, and the produce department seemed particularly grim.

"Excuse me," she said to a young man in a long white apron putting the offending apples on display, "but don't you have any other apples?"

He shook his head.

"Well, my goodness, these are so tiny and

ugly. Where are all the nice big, shiny red ones?"

Looking her over carefully, he answered in a flat voice, "They haven't been born yet."

"I beg your pardon?"

His expression clearly said, Spare me from private-school students. Aloud, he said, "Not the right time of year, miss. Not many apple trees blooming in early spring, you know? That doesn't happen until summer." A wicked grin teased at his mouth.

Jane flushed. She knew she was being ridiculed. "Well, of course!" she said stiffly. "I just thought you might have apples shipped in from someplace else."

"Yup, we do. But the sunny south had a bad winter. Was in *all* the papers."

Now what? Meredith was counting on her. Such a simple errand: buy what was on the list. Well, Meredith hadn't actually *ordered* her to buy it all here, in this store. There are other stores in town, Jane thought, making up her mind. I'll buy the ketchup and mustard and mayonnaise here, because who cares about that stuff? But I'll get the bread at the bakery down the street, the cold cuts at the meat market, and the fruits at that darling little specialty shop on the corner. The only two things they sold that were edible were fruit and candy, so the fruit would almost certainly be of the finest quality.

The condiments she bought failed to make much of a dent in her supply of cash. Meredith had given her plenty of money. She stuffed the bills back into her purse.

Ten minutes later, she left the bakery in a state of shock. How could something as basic as bread cost so much money? And she'd had to buy so many loaves! The bakery owner had been thrilled. It was, she had said as she bustled about collecting every loaf of bread in the place, about time Canby Hall threw some business her way. She couldn't understand why they hadn't done it long ago.

Jane did, the minute she saw the bill. She fingered her diminished pile of bills as she headed for the meat market. It wasn't as if she intended to buy roast beef or leg of lamb. Those things probably cost a fortune. But cold cuts weren't really *meat*, were they? Probably they were just leftover pieces of the more expensive cuts of meat, they couldn't cost much, could they?

Yes, they could, as it turned out. As a very happy butcher called out to Jane her promise to deliver the goods that very afternoon. She left the meat market with a queasy feeling in the pit of her stomach. She still hadn't bought fruits or vegetables, and all of Meredith's money was gone. Fortunately, she had money of her own. Thank goodness she'd had the presence of mind to bring it with her. And there was always the little plastic card in her wallet. Several of them, in fact.

"Food just should *not* be so expensive," she muttered as she hurried to the specialty shop.

"It's criminal!" Paying a lot for a cashmere sweater was one thing, because you had it until you got good and tired of it or accidentally got ink on an elbow or cuff. But food, well, that was *gone* in a meal or two and then where were you? You just had to go out and buy it all over again.

Shaking her head, Jane went into the little shop, decorated like a country store, and headed straight for a bushel basket chock-full of nice big, shiny red apples. In her right hand she clutched a small plastic card. They would take a credit card, wouldn't they?

They would. And they did. But that still left her with one tiny little problem. They had huge baskets of apples and oranges (*orange* ones), but no vegetables. And hadn't they promised Ms. Allardyce that they'd all eat lots of veggies? She had no choice. She would have to swallow her pride and return to the supermarket. She'd have to use her own money.

She grabbed lettuce, tomatoes, onions, cucumbers, and carrots. Waiting outside for Meredith, Jane felt very nervous, as if she'd done poorly on an exam. True, she'd purchased everything on the list and had arranged for everything but the vegetables, which she was carrying in two large grocery bags, to be delivered. Mission accomplished. So why was her stomach jumping hurdles?

She'd spent far too much money. She knew it. She should have bought every single thing right here at the supermarket. But then, she shouldn't have come in the first place. Meredith shouldn't have picked her, of all people! What did *she* know about grocery-shopping?

She giggled, thinking of how surprised the cooks would be when the bakery truck, the meat market truck, and the specialty shop van all pulled up in front of the dining hall.

And she did more than giggle when Meredith, after loading the bags of vegetables into the car and climbing into the front seat, held out a hand and asked, "Any change?" Jane laughed hilariously. Then, as they drove toward Canby Hall in the gathering dusk, Jane told Meredith what she'd done.

"I feel so totally stupid," she finished as Meredith listened silently. "I just had no idea stuff could cost so much." She hesitated and then added, "I let you down and I'm sorry."

"It's my fault," her housemother said as they rounded a curve in the road. "I should have known you'd have trouble with the food at the supermarket. This is a bad time of year for produce, but I was hoping you'd get lucky. I should have told you that if the supply of fresh vegetables was really atrocious, to go for canned or frozen fruit for now."

Canned fruit! Frozen fruit! The thought hadn't even entered Jane's mind.

Meredith smiled over at her. "Learn anything?" she asked gently.

"Yes," Jane said firmly, "I learned never to

go food shopping without a credit card." They both laughed and then she added more seriously, "Really, Merrie, I hope you'll give me another chance. I know I messed up today, but I'd like to try it again. If you'll give me some tips first."

Merrie reached over and patted her arm. "Of course, Jane. It takes time to learn basic things, just as it does your studies. Actually, although I know this strike is a nuisance for you girls, I wonder if it might not be a blessing in disguise. After all, it's giving all of you an opportunity to learn things you haven't come up against before."

Jane made a face. "Maybe it's not safe to let us do these things. Aren't you afraid we'll accidentally burn down the Dining Hall?"

"The time to do that," Merrie said with a straight face, "was *before* we changed the menus."

They were both still laughing when they pulled up in front of Baker House. "I'll drop you off here," Meredith said, "and then I'll take these groceries over to Dining Hall. See you later."

Jane was so glad Meredith wasn't angry with her, she wasn't prepared for how angry Cary was.

"What's the big idea, running out on us like that?" he demanded, his arms full of tools. The dimming daylight made it impossible to work any longer, and he was on his way to Baker's basement to store them.

"I had an errand to run for Meredith," Jane said loftily, neglecting to add that she'd botched the errand. He already seemed to think she was incapable of doing anything really important.

Andy joined them, saving Jane from any detailed explanation as to her whereabouts. "I need a couple of people to help me and Dee lug the dunk tank liner up from the basement. It's too heavy for one person."

Two of the boys from Ambulance volunteered, as did Matt. Jane filled her arms full of tools and followed along. They found the metal tank, covered with cobwebs, sitting in a corner of Baker House's basement. It was small, but round and solid, though surprisingly lightweight.

When they reached their work spot, they dumped the tank on the ground. "Now the question is," Andy remarked, "who knows how the dunking mechanism works?"

Her companions stared at her.

"I mean," she said with a little laugh, "I don't really think people will pay to see someone sitting on a little platform. They pay to see someone hit the drink, right? Which is why they throw the softball at the little lever."

"Lever?" Dee asked.

"Yes, you know . . . that little round handle people toss the ball toward. It's what makes the seat drop into the water."

"Seat?" This from Maggie. "Andy, I've never been to a carnival before. I don't know anything about the dunk tank. Or the seat. Or the lever."

"Well, who does?" Andy looked around the group expectantly. In the falling darkness, she could just barely make out a complete lack of expression on every face.

"Maybe there are instructions in that black notebook," Matt suggested. "Take a look."

"Well, I can't *see*. It's getting too dark. If all the tools are put away, let's go over to Baker and take a look at the notebook there."

When they were all seated in the first-floor parlor, Andy leafed through the pages until she found the right one. "Here it is!" she cried, removing a sheet and handing it to Matt. "See? It says right here: 'dunk tank mechanism.'"

Matt stared at it. "Andy," he said after a long minute, "this looks like hieroglyphics to me. It might as well be written in sanskrit."

"But you're going to be an engineer! If you can't read those plans, who can?"

"Andy, I'm going to be an electrical engineer. Do you see any lights on this diagram?"

"Jane?" she asked with hope in her voice.

Jane gave the plans a quick glance before shaking her head. "Whoever designed this did it for their own benefit, not someone else's. All these little squiggles and numbers wouldn't mean a thing to anyone but them. Why don't you just ask one of your *friends* on your precious picket line?"

"Hey, Jane," Cary began, but to everyone's

surprise, Andy threw her arms around Jane's
neck and cried, "Of course! Why didn't I
think of that? Jane, you're a genius! Even if
Leo didn't draw up these plans, he'll know
who did. Thanks!"

She was about to run out of the building,
plans in hand, when Matt stopped her. "Andy,
forget it for today. The strikers have all gone
home to eat, which is what we should all be
doing. My poor, tired body is screaming,
'Feed me, feed me!' I'm out of here, and you
guys better head for the Dining Hall or you'll
miss dinner."

Andy sagged in disappointment. "Okay, I
guess you're right," she said reluctantly. "It
can wait until tomorrow. We couldn't do
anything with it tonight, anyway. And we
did get a lot done today."

"Well, come on, then," Dee urged, heading
for the door. "It's probably just a wild rumor,
but I heard they might actually be serving
something edible tonight. Something about
new menus. I can't figure out which I feel the
most, curiosity or terror."

Jane kissed Cary good-bye and smiled to
herself. She knew everyone was in for a
pleasant surprise tonight. Enjoy it while you
can, she thought as they walked across campus,
because you will never eat this well at Canby
Hall again. My credit card couldn't take the
strain!

CHAPTER ELEVEN

The new menus were a big hit, as much for ease of clean-up as for improvement in taste.

"Okay," Andy told the girls at her table, "we've given everyone a treat, right? Now we're going to ask for payment." Standing on her chair, she clanked a plastic cup with a fork until she had everyone's attention. "Okay, everybody, lend me your ears!"

Expectant silence filled the room. Crunching, munching, and sipping came to a halt. Knowing that they were all hoping she was about to announce an end to the strike, Andy hurried her words. "Listen, guys, I don't know about Addison and Charles, but Baker House looks like a freight train tore through it. We're not keeping our bargain with P.A."

A girl at the next table called, "Who died and left *you* boss?" Her companions nodded. "You're not even our housemother. Why don't you just take care of Baker and let the rest of us alone?"

Andy had expected that. "Because we're all in this together. When we promised Ms. Allardyce that we'd take care of things, we promised for everyone."

"Well, maybe you shouldn't have," a dark-haired girl sitting at a far table yelled. "I'm sick to death of cleaning and dusting. At least the staff got paid for doing all that grungy stuff!"

There was a chorus of disgruntled "Yeah's!"

Andy shook her head. "It's for everyone's benefit. If the school closes, we'll all have to go home."

"Great!" someone cried. "I could use the rest." Other voices mumbled agreement.

Andy stood her ground. "Oh, right. And you'll all simply love going to school in the summer, right? Instead of swimming and surfing and camping and whatever else you do in the summertime."

Ride my horse, Toby thought.

Lie by the pool, Jane thought, picturing herself with a golden tan.

Surf and hang out on the beach, Dee thought, a dreamy expression on her face.

"Besides," Andy continued, knowing she'd made them stop and think, "the carnival is important, you all know that. It brings in money for the school. If we go home, the carnival will be canceled."

No one said anything. She shifted from one

foot to the other and took a deep breath. "Now! Are we going to clean up our act? And our houses?"

A chorus of groans followed, but no one protested. "C'mon, guys," Andy continued, softening her voice. "We can do this, I know we can." She grinned. "It'll be good for us. You never know when you might need to know how to turn on a dishwasher or slap a mop around a kitchen floor, right?"

The silence was stunning.

"It's just a matter of getting organized, that's all," Andy said. "And if you have any questions about how to do something, ask your housemother. She'll know how. Or ask one of the girls who looks like she knows how. They'll show you. After all, we're all in this together."

"Tell them no more green sheets!" Jane hissed, tugging at Andy's sweater sleeve. Andy waved her away.

"Okay, so we're going to give it all we've got, right?"

Reluctant nods bobbed around the room.

"Good! Now, about the carnival . . ."

It was dark when they left the Dining Hall. They had left behind two very pleased cooks. "The menus, at least," Toby said, "were a big hit with everyone."

"Yeah," Andy agreed. "I wish I could say the same for my pep talk. Everybody was looking at me like I had a whip in one hand and a chair in the other."

"Well," Toby said staunchly, "since Baker House looked like animals lived there, maybe animal training equipment wouldn't be such a bad idea."

"I know, but I think I came on a little strong. I'll probably be treated like the enemy tomorrow."

"No, you won't. Everyone knows you were just thinking of the school." Toby loved walking across campus at night. She especially loved this new springtime. Lights from the brick dorm buildings cast a soft glow over the delicate, lacy new green on the huge old trees. And although two girls in her science class insisted spring had no special smell, Toby disagreed. She was convinced she could smell green grass growing, leaves budding overhead, and flowers opening in their beds. It was all so different from spring in the Texas hill country, and she loved it. Especially at night.

"You *did* come on a little strong," Jane told Andy, a hint of resentment in her voice. They reached Baker House and went inside. "I mean, it's not like you're class president or something."

Andy groaned silently as they went up the stairs. "Sorry, Jane," she said guiltily. "I guess I should have let you give the lecture. But look at it this way, I really did you a favor. I mean, now everyone thinks *I'm* too bossy, not you." She grinned. "Wasn't that nice of me?"

Jane and Toby laughed. And Toby added,

"Well, whatever they think, your little speech must have done some good." Baker House was humming with activity. There were girls everywhere, armed with mops and dust rags and bottles of glass cleaner. One of the mop-wielding girls waved a greeting. "We decided you were right," she called. "Nobody wants to sit in a hot classroom this summer."

Although none of the girls from 407 were on the evening chore charts, they decided to get into the spirit of things by cleaning their own room. Jane protested mildly at first, but since there was no room left on her nightstand to put anything, she decided cleaning was a good idea.

"Just get a big plastic bag," Toby suggested dryly, "and dump your whole corner into it."

"Even my bed?"

"Well, at least then you wouldn't have to worry about getting those yucky green sheets again."

When they had finished and even Jane's corner was neat, they grabbed their robes and headed for the bathroom. The halls were quiet (and clean) now. "It'll be nice to walk into a shiny bathroom for a change," Jane said cheerfully. "Donna and Teresa were in here earlier tonight, scrubbing away. Glad it wasn't *me*."

She reached the bathroom door first, and promptly stepped into a thin stream of water trailing lazily across the hall floor. She was wearing flat sandals on her feet and as the water oozed across her bare toes, she looked down in amazement. "There is not supposed to be water on this floor," she said clearly.

Toby and Andy looked down at Jane's feet. "I think," Toby said, "that it's coming from the bathroom."

"Oh, no," Andy murmured, and yanked open the bathroom door. "Well," she said after a minute as Jane and Toby peeked around her shoulder, "at least it's clean!"

It *was* clean. There were no wet towels on the floor, the mirrors were free of soap scum, the sinks shining. But there was a problem: Someone had failed to completely turn off a faucet, which wouldn't have been a disaster if the drain in that sink had been open. It wasn't. A thin but steady stream of water was flowing into the sink and slopping over the sides onto the floor, where it spread evenly over the white tiles and underneath the door into the hall.

Silence filled the bathroom, broken only by the steady drip of water hitting the tiles. "We'd better go get mops," Toby said wearily. "I know at least one girl down on the third floor who never learned how to swim."

They turned to wade to the broom closet. Suddenly, Jane stopped. "No," she said. "No."

Andy and Toby turned to stare at her. "No what?"

"No, we are not going to mop this up."

"We're not?"

"No. What good was that speech you made

tonight in the Dining Hall if we clean up after someone else's mistake? I'm going to get Teresa and Donna. Let them clean this up." And she sloshed out of the room.

They waited. A few minutes later, the door swung open and in came Jane, hands clutching the elbows of two very sleepy girls in pajamas and robes and slippers.

"We were in *bed*," the shorter of the two girls moaned. "She got us out of *bed*! I was almost asleep!"

"I don't care," Jane retorted. "We're tired, too. You made this mess, now you just clean it up."

Seeing Jane impersonating an angry parent sent Toby and Andy into giggles. "Gosh," Andy said admiringly, "how do you know how to do that?"

"Andy," Jane said sternly, "you are *not* helping." To the guilty parties, Jane ordered, "Go get mops from the broom closet. The sooner you start, the sooner you'll be back in your nice, warm beds."

Still protesting, the girls slouched off. When they had returned armed with mops and Jane was finally convinced they would do the job necessary, she and her roommates returned to 407.

"At least we know the bathroom will be clean!" Toby said as she flung herself across her bed.

"Now if it would only stay that way," Jane commented, unwrapping a candy bar. "Well,

we can at least keep our own room clean."
Even as she spoke the words, she tossed the
candy wrapper onto her nightstand. Toby
knew that it would stay right there until their
next heavy-duty cleaning session.

"What is needed in this world," Andy announced as she reached under her bed for her
latest goodie box from home, "is a high-gloss
super spray to preserve a clean room." She
sat up, two shiny red apples in hand. "You'd
get the room all nice and sparkly and then
spray it with this stuff and the room would
stay that way forever."

Toby accepted the apple Andy offered her.
"Well," she said before taking a healthy bite,
"you'd have to spray the *people* into place,
too, because they're the ones who mess everything up." Her green eyes focused directly on
Jane.

Jane flushed, grabbed the candy wrapper
and, raising an arm, tossed it into the wastebasket at the foot of Andy's bed with the pre-
cision of a basketball pro.

Her roommates cheered and clapped.

Jane wasn't too tired to stand up and take
a bow.

CHAPTER TWELVE

The next day, they went straight to the work site after classes. The boys from Oakley Prep arrived minutes later.

"Nothing like the smell of fresh-cut lumber," Matt said happily as he slid one sheet of wood onto the tarp-covered ground.

Andy nodded. "It does smell good." But she was too busy studying the dunk tank instructions to concentrate on anything else. It looked so complicated.

"I'm going to go find Leo," she announced, "and see if he can translate any of this for us."

She was back fifteen minutes later, a gleeful grin on her face. Waving the sheet of paper in the air, she cried triumphantly, "By George, I think I've got it! It's a cinch, honest! Leo explained it all and it's as easy as pie. No problem!"

Matt wasn't so sure. When she explained what the diagram symbols meant, he said slowly, "Well, we'll give it a try. But the last time somebody told me putting something together was as easy as pie, the handlebars on my bicycle pointed backwards."

Andy laughed. "The dunk tank doesn't have any handlebars," she pointed out, "so quit worrying."

Matt shrugged and went back to sawing. Andy surveyed the scene before her, smiling with satisfaction. Spring sunshine shone down on a hubbub of activity all across campus. Along with the busy construction crew, there were Canby Hall girls sweeping the walks, tending the flower beds and washing windows. She was convinced they were going to pull this off, after all. They would have their carnival.

"I'm going to get the hoses," she told Matt. "You guys are almost finished with the frame for the dunk tank. I need to make sure it doesn't have any leaks. Be right back!" And she ran off again, half-skipping, half-jumping with her dancer's grace.

"Well," Jane remarked, handing Cary the nail he'd asked for, "at least she's not playing waitress for those strikers again."

Cary looked up from the slice of lumber Matt was holding steady for him. "Why does it bother you that Andy's being nice to the people on the picket line?"

To Jane, something in his voice felt like fingernails scraping across a blackboard. "I . . . I didn't mean anything," she said quickly. She did *not* want to fight with Cary on such a beautiful day. It was bad enough that the only time they saw each other these days was during a work session. If things stayed this way much longer, she wouldn't even recognize Cary unless he had a hammer or saw in his hands. "I just meant . . ."

He turned away from her, saying over his shoulder, "You just meant Andy should be treating people on the picket line the same way you do — as if they don't exist. You don't have the faintest notion of what kind of problems those people have and you never will." His voice had risen and to Jane's ears, it seemed magnified. To her horror, she realized hammers and saws had stopped. People were listening.

"That's not fair!" she protested. "You don't know any more about their problems than I do. No one at Canby or Oakley does. So why are you sounding so superior, like you grew up with those people and know all about them? You grew up, Cary Slade, with people like *me*."

"Well, at least I'm keeping an open mind. So is Andy. Yours is shut tighter than a pickle-jar lid."

His tone was final, dismissing her. Hearing it, the embarrassed workers returned to their tasks, while Jane sat silently, her cheeks scarlet. She sank back on her heels, pretending to be fascinated by a bright yellow flower in the grass. Cary really wasn't being fair. She wasn't the same kind of person as Andy, and she'd never pretended to be. And it seemed very perverse of Cary, who had put his entire family in an uproar by insisting on being different, to now suggest that *she* be just like Andy. Why couldn't she be different, too?

She picked up a hammer and began pounding, in a rhythm that matched the angry pounding of her heart.

Unaware that she had been indirectly responsible for another Cary-Jane confrontation, Andy was experiencing her own problems. She had expected her errand to be such a simple matter: Go into the basement, take the hose down from its hanger on the wall, and lug it upstairs. No big deal.

But just getting the thick rubber coils off the wall required a bit of ingenuity, because the hook on which it hung was too high above her head. She had to stretch to her full height to be able to touch the wall rack. And being able to touch it wouldn't do the trick. She had to be able to unhook the hose from the rack.

Pulling an old wooden chair over underneath the rack, she climbed up on it. Thus positioned, she reached up to lift the coiled hose from its rack. But it was too heavy to lift in one solid coil. It might as well have been a truckload of bricks. Andy had the eerie sensation that it had been lying in wait for her all day to destroy her sense of well-being. "Well, it's working," she told the immobile hose with her nastiest glare. "You're ruining my good mood. But I refuse to let anything made of red rubber defeat me."

Reaching up deliberately, she unwound it, letting it drop, loop by loop, to the floor. That done, she jumped down from the chair. "Now what?" she asked the unwound hose, lying peacefully on the cement floor. "If I coil you nice and neat, you'll be too heavy to carry." She sighed. "I guess I'll just have to drag you."

That, she quickly discovered, was easier said than done. Parts of the hose kept catching on edges of boxes, on the furnace pipes, and on the stairs when she got to them. After wrestling with the length of hose for five very long minutes, during which time she tripped twice on a coil and would have fallen to the floor if she hadn't grabbed the stair railing for support, she threw the hose nozzle to the floor, crying, "Oh, all right, you win! I hate to admit it, but you're too much for me. I'm going for help." She pointed down at the pale red hose, lying in a twisted-pretzel heap at her feet. "Do not," she warned, "move one single inch while I'm gone! I'll be right back with reinforcements."

Then, although she felt silly about the whole thing, she ran up the stairs to get Matt.

"Wow!" he declared when he saw the tangled mess on the basement floor, "you did this all by yourself? Congratulations!"

"Ma-at! The thing has a mind of its own,

honest! I don't see why Canby Hall couldn't afford one of those newer light plastic green ones, instead of this heavy, old-fashioned one."

To her supreme satisfaction, Matt didn't get along any better with the hose than she had. When he tried to wind it one way, it chose to curl itself tightly in the opposite direction. When he stepped into the center of the pile to search for an end, red tentacles seemed to wind themselves around his ankles. He moaned with frustration.

Andy giggled. "Wish I had a camera. This would make a great movie. 'Attack of the Red Rubber Hose.'"

"Very funny. How about helping me out here instead of amusing yourself at my expense?"

"Okay, okay. Where's your sense of humor?" Grinning slyly, she said, "Maybe the hose drained it out of you," and then laughed hilariously. "Get it? Hose? Drained?"

"*Andy!*"

"Oh, all right. Grouch." She stepped into the center of the pile to help him search for an end to the hose. They found one, and as she pulled on that end, he fed the hose to her, smoothing kinks and curls as they made their way toward the stairs.

After a great deal of pulling and tugging, they made it up the stairs and to the front door of Baker House with their unwieldy prize. "I'll hook it up to the outside faucet,"

Andy volunteered. "You take the other end over to the dunk tank, okay?"

Matt nodded agreement. "I think they've got the tank framed in. They're still working on the dunking mechanism. Toby thinks she's figured it out, though. Might be ready to try out by the time you get the tank filled."

It was. And to everyone's astonishment, it was Jane who insisted on being the first volunteer to test the lever. She said it was because she was hot and the water would cool her off.

"It'll be awfully cold, Jane," Andy warned. "The sun hasn't had a chance to warm up the water yet. And it's getting chilly out here now."

"It'll be invigorating," Jane insisted, climbing up the wooden steps Matt had fashioned out of lumber. "I'll just pretend I'm a member of that Polar Bear Club that swims in the Atlantic Ocean in January. Who knows, after this maybe they'll make me an honorary member." She reached out over the tank to pull on the rope holding the swing, drawing the swing toward her. The rope and the swing were suspended from a sturdy metal canopy Cary had attached to the sides of the tank, according to the directions scribbled on the paper. Swing in hand, Jane asked Cary and Matt to hold it while she climbed on. That done, she held both sides of the swing's ropes and called out cheerfully, "Okay, who just can't wait to make me look like a wet duck?"

No one volunteered. Their expressions admitted that they just couldn't imagine Jane Barrett looking anything less than perfect. And no one wanted to be responsible for such a drastic change of image.

Jane laughed. "Oh, come on, you guys! We have to find out if this thing works, don't we? Why not me? I promise I won't dissolve when I hit the water." Although she sounded cheerful, Jane was beginning to fear that they wouldn't let her do this. And she wanted to. She needed to. She wanted to feel she was part of all this, the way Andy was, the way Matt and Cary were, and Dee and Maggie, and all the others. She hated feeling separate from everybody else.

She fixed her blue eyes on Andy's face and sent her a silent one-word message. The word was, *Please!*

And because Andy knew Jane better than anyone else, even Cary, she understood exactly what Jane was trying to do.

"I'll go first," she said. "What are friends for?"

Cary shrugged and handed her the softball. Everyone moved back to give Andy pitching room. The sun's last rays faded and a chilly breeze drifted across campus. Jane, her feet just above the water, shivered, although the pink sweatsuit was warm enough.

"You sure about this?" Andy called, seeing her shiver.

"I'm sure. And I'm not the least bit worried. I've seen you throw a ball in gym class. You couldn't hit the lever with a basketball!"

The words were barely out of her mouth when the softball hit the round metal lever with a sharp clunk. The seat went down and Jane went with it, sliding into the cold water with a shocked gasp. A loud cheer rose from the crowd.

Bobbing back up to the surface, Jane heard the cheer. Hair and clothing sodden, eyes wide, she couldn't be sure if the cheer was for her or for the successful dunking mechanism. But she didn't really care. She was freezing and intensely uncomfortable, as Matt, Andy, and Cary helped her out of the water, but she'd never felt better in her life. Hadn't she just done what nobody else wanted to do?

"You didn't have to do that," Cary said softly, removing his plaid shirt and wrapping it around her.

"No?" she asked lightly, smiling up at him. "Gee, I thought I did. How else could I get my honorary membership in the Polar Bear Club?" But she was shivering even as she said it, her teeth chattering together with a rhythmic click-click sound.

"Well," Andy said brightly, "thanks to Jane, we know the dunking mechanism works. We did it!"

Everyone cheered again and Jane cheered loudest of all, in spite of her chattering teeth.

CHAPTER THIRTEEN

Satisfied that there were no leaks in the dunk tank, Andy and Matt covered it with one of the tarpaulins. Then, while Jane ran inside to dry off and change her clothes, they carted the hose back to Baker House. Toby thought about hiking over to the Crowell ranch, but decided against it. If there were no clean towels, Jane would shriek.

"How about some pizza?" Matt asked Andy as they reached the top of the basement stairs at Baker. "We've earned it, right?"

"Right! Listen, we should put this hose back on its rack. But that would mean another wrestling match that could take hours. Let's do it later. For now, just give it a heave down the stairs. I'm starving."

Because he was just as hungry as she was, Matt didn't argue. The hose half-slid, half-flew down the stairs, landing in a jumbled heap near the furnace. To Andy, it looked like one giant, fat worm lying there. Shivering in distaste, she closed the basement door. "C'mon, let's go!"

When they were seated in a window booth at Pizza Pete's, Matt said, "Think we'll ever get this carnival off the ground?"

Andy stared through the glass into the surrounding darkness. The smell of baking pizza made her stomach ache. Pizza Pete's was crowded with local public school students, talking and laughing.

Sighing, Andy said, "Sure. We'll get it going. We've made lots of progress already." But even to her own ears, her voice sounded tired and weak. As if, she thought, I'd just run a long race. When in truth, the race isn't even half-over yet!

Matt said nothing as their waitress plunked their pizza, steaming hot, on the table. "You don't sound too sure," he said when she'd gone. "Things not going too well at Canby? I know you've all got a lot to do." He laughed lightly. "To hear Jane tell it, you're all slaving away."

Andy grinned as she blew on a slice of pizza to cool it. "To hear *Jane* tell it, she's running the school single-handedly. She'll probably write a novel about it one day and the only character in the whole book will be Jane. She could title it, *Me, Myself, and I at Canby Hall*.

Matt laughed. "Seriously," he said then, leaning forward, his dark eyes sincere, "how *is* it going?"

Andy shook her head and wiped her mouth with a paper napkin. "It could be worse, I guess. Maybe. The thing is, it would be a cinch if more of the girls knew what they were doing." She told him about the green sheets and the bathroom flooding and the petty arguing that went on constantly about who was supposed to do which chores. "When we made out the chore charts," she explained, "we tried really hard to be fair. You know, divide them up so no one had more to do than someone else. But then a lot of the girls left, and that changed everything. And there *are* some girls who don't know how to do any of this stuff. I had never waxed a floor before, Toby had never ironed, and Jane's idea of 'housework' is closing a door behind her when she leaves a room."

Matt laughed. But she looked so distressed, he reached out and took her hand. "Hardly anybody knows how to do *all* of that stuff," he said. "Cheer up!"

Back at Canby Hall, Jane had been pleased to find Cary waiting for her in the lobby of Baker House. She'd dried off and changed into gray flannel trousers, a white blouse, and a pale yellow crew-neck sweater. Finding the blouse hadn't been easy.

"Anybody seen my white blouse?" she yelled down the length of the hall when she discovered it missing from her clean laundry.

An amused Dee peeked around the corner

of the door of Room 409. "How many white blouses do you think there are on this floor, Jane?" she asked. "What does yours look like?"

"It has long sleeves and a Peter Pan collar."

"They *all* have long sleeves and most of them have Peter Pan collars." Dee wrinkled her nose. "How are we supposed to know which one is yours?"

"It has my *name* in it, of course."

"Oh." Dee, who had neglected to obey the rule about labeling all garments, looked properly chastened. "Well, then, where did you see it last?"

"It was in the laundry. I put it there yesterday morning."

Dee laughed, as Maggie joined her to see what was going on. "Yesterday morning? And you expect it to be washed, dried, starched, and ironed within twenty-four hours? Good grief, Jane, you must think you're at home. You'll be lucky if you get that blouse back by the end of the term."

Jane frowned and fiddled with the belt on her white robe. "But the laundry is always back within twenty-four hours."

"Not lately, it isn't. Haven't you noticed? And besides, Jane, this isn't always. This is during a strike. We always got the clothes back really fast because the laundry workers knew what they were doing. But in case you haven't noticed, they're not here now. They're out on the picket line. You'd better forget about that blouse and wear something else."

Jane's lower lip jutted forth. "I *always* wear that blouse with my yellow sweater."

"There you go again with that word always. Haven't you been listening to me?" Dee grinned. "I mean, it's not like you don't *own* another white blouse, Jane. We all know better than that."

Her amusement infuriated Jane. "Oh, I hate this stupid strike!" she shouted. Then she turned on her heel and went back inside her room, slamming the door behind her.

Several minutes later, as she was rummaging through the closet for a replacement for the missing white blouse, a knock sounded on the door. She opened it to find a short, plump girl holding up Jane's white blouse.

"I'm sorry," she said, "but this was sent to my room by mistake. I guess it's yours. Your name's in it. But you'd better check it out before you put it on. Two of my skirts came back from the laundry with broken zippers and one of my sweaters turned a dreadful shade of green."

"Must have been in the same load as my sheets," Jane murmured.

"Pardon?"

"Nothing. Listen, thanks for delivering it. I appreciate it."

Sure enough, when the girl had gone, Jane discovered a button missing. But since she was wearing the blouse under a sweater, she decided to wear it anyway and hope she wouldn't get struck by a car and have to go to the hospital, where the missing button would surely be discovered.

"I just think this whole ridiculous strike business has gone on long enough!" she complained to Cary as they walked across campus toward the wishing well. It was one of Jane's favorite spots on campus. This night was especially nice, Jane thought, in spite of her bad mood. The navy blue sky overhead was free of clouds and liberally sprinkled with stars, and a warm breeze chased Cary's blond bangs across his forehead.

"Can we not discuss the strike?" he asked, taking her hand in his. "We'll just get into an argument. And I do *not* want to argue with you tonight."

Jane knew he was right. They'd spent so little time alone lately. They could sit beside the wishing well and talk about normal, nice things. Like how glad they were that spring was finally here, and how lucky they were to be attending schools so close to each other, and didn't Andy and Matt make a nice couple? They could have a nice, quiet hour or so together.

So why did Cary's sharpness with her that afternoon keep popping into her mind? She didn't *want* it to. She tried to keep it out. After all, he had waited for her in the lobby all that time while she searched for the blouse.

But as hard as she tried, Jane couldn't erase the unpleasant image of everyone staring at

her when Cary ordered, yes, *ordered* her to
go get cold drinks for everyone. And he'd
been cross with her because she didn't return
with the drinks. Even after she'd explained
that Merrie had asked her to run an errand,
that unfair scowl had stayed right there on his
great-looking face. As if she'd abandoned all
of those thirsty people on purpose. Cary, Jane
decided, would never learn the details of her
disastrous shopping trip. That was all he'd
need to get him started on another lecture
about her helplessness.

"Cary," her mouth was saying even as her
brain was saying, Jane, do not do this, "I
don't understand why you were so rude to me
today in front of everybody. It was excruciat-
ingly embarrassing."

He let go of her hand.

"Okay, Jane," he said, stopping in his tracks
under an old maple tree, "you just won't
be satisfied until we hassle, will you? I defended Andy today because she was right and
you were wrong. Got that? And I'll do it again
tomorrow if you make any cracks about Andy
being nice to the strikers."

"I wasn't even talking about that," she said.
"I was talking about your ordering me
around. But since you mentioned it, why *do*
you have to take Andy's side?" She stood
stiffly, chin raised, arms at her side. "You
don't even know any of those people on the
picket line."

"I know they're *people*. That's all I need

to know. Andy knows it, too. And that's the way she treats them. You might try it some time."

"And you might try understanding how I feel, too!" she flared. "This whole thing has just turned everything upside-down. And I don't see what good it's doing anyone."

"You wouldn't," Cary said flatly. He looked down at her and she could feel his eyes on her face. "If you would, just once, try to put yourself in someone else's shoes. It's not that hard, Jane. And you'd learn a lot."

Sometimes, she thought, Cary Slade could be positively insufferable. This was one of those times. "Then put yourself in *my* shoes. Try cleaning a bathroom and organizing a carnival and keeping up with your schoolwork!" His outraged silence told her she'd hit close to home.

"C'mon," he finally said flatly, "I gotta get back. I'll walk you back to Baker, then I'm splitting."

Are you satisfied? she asked herself. She tried to think of some way to salvage the evening, but she knew it was no use. Cary had made up his mind to cut the evening short and nothing would change it now. And she certainly wasn't going to beg. Barretts did not beg. And regardless of what he felt about the strike, it didn't justify his being rude to her.

"Fine," she said curtly. She whirled around and headed across campus. Neither of them said a word.

CHAPTER
FOURTEEN

For the next two days there were morning chores, classes all day, then work on the carnival before dinner and evening chores. Bodies were weary and tempers were short. In spite of Jane's disapproval, Andy continued to visit the picket line with cold drinks or coffee and cookies. The more time she spent talking with the strikers, the more she understood their problems, which unleashed a whole new set of arguments between her and Jane. If they had a good day, where few things went wrong, the subject didn't come up. But on those days when the plumbing threw a tantrum or the washing machine burped too many suds, Jane blamed the strikers and Andy immediately defended them.

Toby got so tired of hearing them argue, she grabbed at the chance to do outside chores when her turn arrived. On Saturday, dressing in old clothes she hurried outside. Since she had no classes, she could take her time. Later, everyone would arrive to begin carnival work. But for now, she had the campus all to herself and she was going to enjoy it.

There wasn't that much work to do. The tulip and daffodil beds needed weeding. And Merrie had asked her to cut enough blooms to make several bouquets, to make the beds look neater, and at the same time to brighten up the Dining Hall and Ms. Allardyce's office. When Toby had finished sprucing up the beds, she would water them. But a struggle with the old hose wasn't necessary. Each bed had its own sprinkler system: a pair of faucet-like appendages sticking up out of the soil. All she had to do was turn them on and then, when the soil was thoroughly damp, turn them off.

And she would think and dig at the same time. Kneeling down beside the bed of black tulips Ms. Allardyce cherished, Toby thought about the situation on campus. She yanked at a weed and wondered what her father would have to say about the problems Canby Hall was facing. He didn't, she knew, have much experience with labor problems. But he had common sense.

"Toby," he'd probably say, maybe while he was leaning against a porch post, "seems to me this isn't your problem to wrestle with. Don't go gettin' all tied up in knots over somethin' you can't fix."

And he'd be right, of course. How could

she fix it? She couldn't order the trustees to give back the workers' hours. She could hardly arrange a meeting between the trustees and the strikers. Gosh, she thought as she dug carefully around a clump of tulips, I can't even do anything about Andy and Jane arguing about the strike! And she wondered how they were getting along without her to act as buffer.

Not well, she'd have discovered had she returned to the dorm. Jane was cranky because of Cary's behavior the night before. She wasn't quite sure how their romance had become so badly dented, but she was positive the strike was the hammer that had dealt the blow. It did seem to her that Andy could at least understand that and sympathize.

But Andy wasn't the least bit sympathetic. "It's your own fault," she said bluntly when Jane complained yet again about Cary's attitude. "Cary understands why the workers are striking and you won't even try. That's what makes him disgusted."

"I don't see why I need to understand," Jane retorted, brushing her hair up into a ponytail. She had halls to vacuum this morning, not a task she was looking forward to. No Friday night date with Cary hadn't helped her disposition any, and then she'd overslept. In spite of the early morning sunshine streaming in through their window, she felt out of sync with the whole world. "It's really none of my business."

"It's your school, isn't it?" Andy, looking slender and lithe in a yellow leotard under jeans, tucked in the corners of her tailored bedspread.

"I don't own it!" Jane snapped.

"Mmm, well, that surprises me. I thought you Barretts owned just about everything."

"An-dy!"

"Sorry. Forget it. Where's Toby, anyway?"

Tired of arguing, Jane consulted her charts. "Garden duty this morning. She'll like that. Toby was born for the great outdoors. So *she* will at least be in a good mood. Unlike the rest of Room 407."

"Well, one out of three ain't bad," Andy quipped as she left the room to tackle her laundry chores.

At least she had included herself in the two whose moods weren't so good, Jane reflected. Andy was always fair. Consulting the chore charts again, Jane realized with a pleasant jolt that Baker House, at least, was running more smoothly than it had been. No more green sheets, the bathroom was no longer a combat zone, and the Dining Hall had become almost popular, thanks to their idea. There were more and more days when P.A. could have pulled a surprise inspection at this House without getting *too* upset. Maybe, she thought, laying aside the charts, they *could* actually run the school themselves. Wouldn't that just rattle Cary Slade? Then he'd have to treat her with respect and stop making cracks about spoiled, rich girls. After all, she was the one who had organized the work load. That should count for something, especially if things worked well. And right now, Jane thought with satisfaction, it seems that they are working quite well.

Toby had finished weeding all six beds when Randy pulled up with a familiar bang-boom-rattle. "Hi," he called from the cab of his pickup. Jumping down to join her, he said, "I know your social calendar is jammed full at this point, but I thought you might be able to squeeze in a quick ride on Maxine. She's getting real rusty from misuse. And I know she misses you." When Toby glanced around her doubtfully, he added, "It's still early."

"I know, but I haven't watered the beds yet," she said, getting up and slapping dirt from her jeans.

Randy frowned. "That'll take a while, right?"

"No, not really. I just turn on the sprinklers and then I turn them off later."

They both had the same idea at the same time. Randy said it first. "Great! That works out perfectly. You turn them on, I'll drive you to the ranch, we'll ride, and then you can turn them off when I bring you back. The beds will get a good soaking and you'll get some exercise."

That made sense. What was the point in

hanging around campus watching water run? Glad that she'd already accomplished the weeding, Toby accepted the invitation. "Let me just cut some flowers and run them inside. I'll get one of the girls to take them up to Meredith. Then I'll change into my riding boots and be right down.

Randy put the tools back in the shed while Toby sliced tulip and daffodil stems, placing the cut flowers in a basket over one arm. He then helped her turn on the sprinklers and waited while she ran to Baker House shouting, "Don't go away!"

I'm so lucky, she thought happily as she slipped on her boots. Who'd have thought I'd find a friend who owned horses here in the East? A very long nine-month school year without ever climbing on a horse would have driven her just about nuts!

Andy, returning from the laundry room, agreed to take the flowers to Meredith. "You're not going to be gone long, are you?" she asked Toby anxiously. "We've still got a lot of work on the carnival, and we need all available hands."

"Oh, gosh, no! Just a quick ride to clear out the cobwebs, that's all. I'll be back before the guys from Oakley get here, probably. Tell Jane for me, okay? So she doesn't fly into a fit thinking I'm goofing off."

"Will do." Andy knew how much Toby needed this outing. She'd worn herself out trying to keep the peace in Room 407. "Have a good time. Just hurry back, okay?"

Watching Toby tuck her red curls into a cowgirl hat with a chin strap, Andy wished she were going some place. *Any* place. She was getting tired of work crews and cleaning crews. All those people! What were the chances that she and Matt could take in a movie that night? After all, they couldn't do any carnival work after dark. If she could finish her evening chores fast enough, maybe he'd be willing to rescue her from Canby Hall for the evening.

"Have fun!" she called as Toby rushed out of the room.

Toby intended to do just that. After checking the sprinklers once more to make sure Ms. Allardyce's precious tulips were getting their drink of water, she climbed into Randy's truck and left campus with a big smile on her face.

Toby felt in control again for the first time in weeks, as she rode Maxine over the hills and through the valleys behind the Crowell ranch, with Randy a short distance behind her. The woods were just beginning to awaken. Small creatures darted in and out among the undergrowth, birds busied themselves overhead, and the sun began to trace shadows across the valley floor. This was where Toby most loved the East.

Hair falling loose from under the hat, Toby

rode .on, the morning breeze stroking her cheeks, green eyes shining.

On campus, Andy walked past a tulip bed and thought to herself that it was getting a nice, thorough soaking. Toby had been on the job early. Good girl! Smiling, Andy hurried on to the Dining Hall where she was meeting Dee and Maggie for breakfast.

Randy led Toby to a spot in the valley that was special to him. A secluded grassy green area semicircled by tall pines, one end lying open to a sparkling creek that wound along the edge of the woods, it was the most peaceful spot he knew. He knew Toby would like it.

"It's beautiful," she breathed, looping Maxine's reins around a tree limb. They walked to a group of smooth gray rocks beside the water and sat down.

"Tell me about Neal," Randy said when they were comfortable. Startled, Toby flushed and looked away. She wasn't used to talking to people about her private life, and certainly not with a boy she'd recently had a crush on.

"I'm really interested," Randy prodded. "I mean, I hardly know him." He grinned as Toby reluctantly faced him. "How can I be sure he's okay for you if you don't fill me in on him?"

More big brother stuff, Toby thought. I should have known. She couldn't help comparing the two of them: Neal, most often dressed in a cashmere sweater and knife-creased slacks, blond hair in place, blue eyes smiling; Randy in plaid shirt, holes in elbows, faded jeans, brown hair blown this way and that by the wind, brown eyes smiling . . . were they really all that different? Randy was older by five years. That seemed to be the crucial difference. Toby was convinced that had he been closer to her own age, he wouldn't be asking her about Neal right now. He'd be asking her for a date.

She told him about Neal. She told him that Neal wasn't a snob at all, in spite of his background, so similar to Jane's. She explained how he seemed to pick up on her feelings, know when she was down. And he knew how to cheer her up, make her laugh when she least felt like it.

"Sounds like you really like the guy," Randy said when she paused. And for just a second, she told herself she heard a faint note of regret in his voice. But that was silly, wasn't it? Because he was the one who had made the decision to treat her like a younger sister. She must have invented the regret in his voice.

"Yeah, I guess I do like him," she answered. And just then a movement in the sparkling creek brought her attention to the water flowing by her feet. The water . . .

"Oh, my gosh!" she cried, jumping to her feet. "The sprinklers! I forgot all about them and we've been gone a long time. The flower beds will be drowned. I've gotta get back!"

Nothing Randy said in an attempt to calm her down worked. She threw herself on Maxine and galloped away.

At the farm, one of the hands generously agreed to care for the horses so that Randy could rush Toby back to campus. She was visibly upset, her green eyes standing out in a very pale face, her mouth tight with anxiety.

In the truck, she kept repeating, "Those beds are like Ms. Allardyce's pets. If I've ruined them, I'll die." Any attempts Randy made to lighten the situation were ignored. He gave up and concentrated on his driving.

The truck came to a screeching halt in front of Baker House. Toby was out and on the ground as if she'd been tossed out. She broke into a run, followed closely by Randy. But as the first bed came into view, her movements slowed, then stopped some distance from the bed. When he reached her, he realized that was as close as she could get.

Someone had shut off the sprinklers for Toby Houston, but they'd done it much too late. The bed, its flowers sad and soggy, was overflowing, surrounded now by a moat of muddy water. Soil already saturated by the rain earlier in the week had shrugged the excess water across the lawn.

"Oh, no," Toby whispered, knowing the other five beds would look identical to this sodden mess. "What have I done?"

CHAPTER FIFTEEN

Toby knew next-to-nothing about flowers. The only reason Jane had given her the assignment was her need to be out-of-doors. So she had no idea if the tulips were drowned forever or just temporarily drenched. And if they *did* recover, would they spring back to life before the headmistress walked by? Toby groaned. If they didn't, her head would be on a platter before the day was through.

"Well," Meredith's voice cut through the silence, "have you come to pay your respects to the dead?" The tone of her voice punched Toby in the chest. Nice, kind Merrie was definitely furious with her — which, as unpleasant as that was, was probably nothing compared to the way Ms. Allardyce would react if she caught a glimpse of the corpses.

Walking around to face Toby, Merrie said, "I looked all over for you when Jane told me this was your responsibility. Where have you been?"

Toby's face felt hot. She wasn't used to being in trouble. While there were those girls at school who delighted in getting into one scrape after another, she had never been among them. The independent streak in her that might have led her into trouble was canceled out by her strong dislike of the spotlight.

"I . . . I'm sorry, Merrie. I just went for a quick ride with Randy, and the time just got away from me."

"You went horseback riding?" Merrie waved an angry hand toward the sodden bed and its surrounding mini-lake. "When you were supposed to be taking care of this?"

Toby's eyes surveyed the damage guiltily. "Well, we were only going to be gone for half an hour," she protested weakly. It sounded pathetic to her own ears. "While the sprinklers were on."

"But you *weren't* gone only half an hour. If Ms. Allardyce sees these beds . . ."

"The sun will dry it all out, won't it?" Toby looked up at the sky, shading her eyes with a cupped hand. It was one way to avoid Merrie's stern gaze.

"You expect Mother Nature to clean up this mess?"

Toby tried a tiny smile. She got no response.

"Well," Meredith said, "it's entirely possible that sooner or later the sun *would* dry up these lakes you've scattered across campus. But I see no reason why you should be allowed

to let the sun do your job. You were totally
irresponsible and may have ruined something
that was very important to another human
being. I'm sure you would take much better
care of a horse that you cared about than you
have these flower beds. Am I right?"

Toby nodded miserably.

"Yes, well, it's important that you learn
respect for other people's property as well as
your own. I want you to get a couple of
buckets from the garden shed and bail out
the excess water in these beds and around
these beds. And get some pruning shears and
cut the worst-looking blooms before your
headmistress notices what's happened to her
flowers."

Bail out the water? Bucket by bucket? That
would take hours! She was supposed to help
with the carnival preparations. "What would
I do with all of those buckets of water?" she
asked, thinking surely Merrie would realize
how ridiculous the idea was. If left alone, the
excess water would just slowly sink into the
ground, wouldn't it? Why go to all that
trouble to move it?

"Take it to the pond at the wishing well."

Toby groaned silently. The wishing well
wasn't that far away if you weren't carrying
two buckets filled with water. But if you were,
it would probably seem to be in the next
county.

"Yes, ma'am," she said stiffly. "I really *am*
sorry," she said softly, and when Merrie didn't

answer, Toby turned away to go get her buckets.

Randy insisted on helping. "It was my fault you were gone so long," he told her, taking one of the plastic pails from her. And although she knew Merrie wouldn't agree, she was grateful for the help.

The worst part was, halfway between the tulip bed and the wishing well was the work site where people were now busy constructing carnival booths. As she approached, holding a full pail with both hands and convinced that her arms were being stretched six inches beyond their normal length, an awkward silence descended over the group.

So. They knew about her carelessness and about this punishment. And judging from the expression on Jane's face, at least one person was thoroughly disgusted with her. And since no one else called out a friendly "hi," Toby assumed the others shared Jane's disgust. It wasn't that they all cared about the tulips. A lot of them probably didn't know a tulip from a tree stump. But they knew she'd had this responsibility and she'd goofed it up. And what's more, now she wasn't available to help *them*, and as Andy had reminded her that very morning, they needed all the help they could get.

Between the two of them, she and Randy were able to clear off most of the excess water lying around the beds, so that unless Ms. Allardyce did more than just pass by, she'd have no reason to suspect that her precious tulips had very nearly died long before their time. Toby's back ached and her arms were wrist-to-shoulder pain. But when she had put the pail away and told Randy a grateful goodbye, she went straight to the work site.

"What can I do to help?" she asked a group of very busy people.

"Here, you can help me," Cary called, and she ran to him gratefully. When she had worked with him for over half an hour, Dee and Maggie began talking to her, and then Andy, and in no time at all, everyone but Jane was treating her as if nothing had happened. She suspected they felt she'd suffered enough. And since she was here now, helping, they weren't going to hold the morning against her. It might take Jane, who had generously given her the outside work to begin with, a little longer.

But it didn't. To Toby's surprise, it was Jane who said, "Here, give me that hammer. You've got blisters on your hands from carrying those pails. You can go get us some cold drinks instead."

"Thanks, Jane," Toby said quietly. That *would* be easier on her hands. She was especially grateful because she could tell that things were not going well between Jane and Cary. He had been working with his back to Jane, ignoring her. That had to hurt. Yet Jane had taken the time to notice Toby's discomfort and take pity on her, when she could just as easily have let her suffer in silence. If I live to be a thousand, Toby thought as she hurried away, I will never understand that girl.

Jane was thinking exactly the same thing about Cary. It wasn't like him to hold a grudge. At least, he never had before. They'd had lots of arguments, usually about their backgrounds. Although they'd been raised pretty much the same way and should have had that in common, their feelings about being privileged differed. Cary hated it, she loved it. It was, she admitted silently, amazing that they'd lasted this long together. Part of the reason they had, though, was that Cary had never held a grudge before. So why was he giving her the silent treatment now? Because of those ludicrous arguments about the stupid strike? It wasn't the first thing they'd ever argued about, and it probably wouldn't be the last. Why was he making such a big deal about it?

Or *would* it be the last? Was that what he had in mind? She could hardly argue with a person who wasn't speaking to her.

She tried. "Cary, could you hand me a bunch of nails, please?"

The nails were handed to her, unaccompanied by so much as a "Sure" or "You bet" or "No trouble, here you are."

She tried again. After all, it was a beautiful Saturday afternoon, with a lovely Saturday evening coming up quickly. "The booths we've finished look just like the ones from last year, don't you think, Cary? Who needs outside help anyway?" Oops, wrong thing to say. She shouldn't have mentioned the striking workers. She wanted to forget their arguments, didn't she?

Whether or not the remark reminded him of their arguing, he remained as silent as the piece of lumber he was measuring.

Glancing over at Matt and Andy, who were chatting amiably as they hammered, Jane felt a pang of envy. Andy and Matt got along like peanut butter and jelly. Cary and I, she thought sadly, are more like my horrid green sheets against my Wedgwood blue walls. We just don't match.

But what did that have to do with feelings? Feelings didn't have anything to do with matching.

She'd try one more time. "Cary, if you don't say at least one word to me," spoken in a low but firm voice, "I'm going to pretend your head is part of a booth and use my hammer on it."

"Violence? You would use violence on a person?" he asked, his back still to her.

"He speaks!" she cried. And because she had heard just a trace of the old warmth in that voice, she leaned closer and teased, "I thought you had laryngitis."

He shook his head, and finally turned to look at her, a trace of a smile on his thin face. "Are you trying to convince me how tough you are? Because I'm not buying it. You've probably never swatted a fly in your whole life."

"Actually," she said, smiling up at him, "we don't allow flies in Boston, you should know that." And it became one of those moments when, although they were standing in the middle of a large group of people and were surrounded by pounding hammers and rasping saws and chattering and laughing, they only saw and heard each other. The fact that that could happen still astonished Jane and made her a little dizzy, as if she'd just taken a roller-coaster ride.

"Truce?" Cary asked gently, his eyes on hers.

"Truce." The sun felt warm on her face. At least, she thought it was the sun.

"Go into town with me tonight?"

"Sure. Only . . ." Jane hesitated and then added, "could we bring Toby, too? She's had a really rotten day. And I know Neal's not coming up this weekend. She'd just be sitting in 407 all alone. Would you mind terribly?"

Cary took her hand. "You're something else, you know that?" But she heard admiration in his voice and knew he wasn't annoyed. "A little while ago, you were ranting and raving about how thoughtless and irresponsible Toby was. Now you want to cheer her up. You amaze me!"

"Well, she made up for that already. And if I'd had to lug those pails of water back and forth in front of everyone, I'd have died of mortification. I just think she's earned some time off tonight. Don't you?"

"Yes. I do. And we have, too. And I don't mind if she comes along. Especially since I know Toby's smart enough to jump right out of the car the minute we get back to Baker House, so I can tell you good-night in privacy. Here she comes now."

Jane felt so good, she would have invited the whole town along if she hadn't known that Cary's generosity had its limits. And Toby's obvious pleasure at being invited added to her feeling of well-being. Maybe, she thought as she handed Cary the necessary nails, maybe this strike isn't so terrible, after all.

Saturday night wasn't terrible, either. Jane, Toby, and Cary drove into the village. Tired of pizza, they ate instead at a small Chinese restaurant, where Jane entertained them by describing the shopping trip she had thought she would never share with Cary. But that seemed silly now. She picked up a fortune cookie and held it between the tips of two fingers. "This," she announced, "costs six for one dollar and fifty cents at the bakery. At the supermarket, you can get six for eighty-nine cents. So," she said with a grin, "unless you are filthy rich, go right past the bakery and straight to the supermarket when you're shopping for food. That's what *I* learned."

"But, Jane," Toby said, laughing, "you *are* filthy rich!"

Jane shook her head. "That is no excuse," she said primly, "for tossing money around carelessly."

Cary hooted, and Jane laughed.

When they left the restaurant, they found Matt and Andy walking through the village, hand-in-hand. "We already saw the movie," Andy explained, "and they won't be changing it for at least another week." She shrugged blue-sweatered shoulders. "Anyway, it's such a great night, who wants to sit inside some musty old theater?"

"With a heavy emphasis on the word 'old,' " Jane agreed. She missed Boston most on Saturday nights and often joked about the village of Greenleaf rolling up its sidewalks at seven o'clock every evening.

"At least this place *has* a theater," Toby said as they walked up the main street. All of the little shops were closed, but there were village residents out strolling. "The closest theater to our ranch is fifty miles away. I don't think my dad's seen a movie in twenty years."

Jane's eyes widened in horror. "Fifty miles?"

Toby nodded. "Fifty miles thataway," she joked.

"You must rent a lot of movies for your VCR."

"My VC-what?" Toby was teasing. She

knew what a video-cassette recorder was, but there was none at the Houston ranch and not likely to be one. Jed Houston didn't even particularly like television, putting it in the same category with jet airplanes and microwave ovens — nice once in a while, but hardly necessary.

Some of the villagers waved and called out Andy's name, but more of them said nothing as the Canby Hall students passed. Those who were silent and directed slightly hostile looks toward the students had all been on the picket line. Their obvious resentment made Jane nervous, and when they had walked the length of the village and back again, she talked everyone into heading back to Baker.

When they arrived, Toby thanked Cary and Jane and discreetly disappeared inside. Running up the stairs, she decided it had been a good day in spite of her carelessness. It would, of course, have been better if Neal had been with her tonight. She missed him. Jane had Cary and Andy had Matt.

Toby grinned as she pushed open the door to Room 407. They were getting good-night kissed, and she wasn't. Maybe that was her real punishment for forgetting the sprinklers.

And maybe tomorrow, she'd give Neal a call.

CHAPTER SIXTEEN

Sunday dawned cold and chilly, bringing old sweaters, suitable for a long work session, out of drawers and closets.

Because Jane didn't own a single sweater that could even remotely be considered for a work session, Andy had loaned her an old orange crewneck. There was a small hole in its right elbow, and it had the same shape as a grocery bag. "I can't believe I'm going to let Cary see me like this. And why on earth," turning toward Andy, "would anyone buy an *orange* sweater?"

"To match orange corduroys," came the cheerful answer.

"Andrea Cord, are you telling me you once went out in public completely dressed in orange?" Jane shuddered at the thought.

"Oh, more than once. Lots of times." Andy grinned. "Can't you tell by looking at that sweater that it's been worn a lot?"

"Well, now that you mention it . . ."

Andy laughed. "Relax, Jane. From the look on your face when you came in last night, you and Cary are getting along just fine. If seeing you in an ancient orange sweater changes his mind, it's not true love. Might as well find out the truth now, right?"

Jane's cheeks were red, but that could have been from the sharp wind blowing across campus as they walked to the Dining Hall. "Well, *you* looked positively idiotic when I came in. Must have been Matt's good-night kiss. And I don't see *you* taking any chances in an old orange sweater."

"How can I? My rich, spoiled roommate is wearing it because she doesn't even *own* anything old enough to grub around in."

"Andy! I'm not spoiled!" But Jane was grinning as she said it.

Toby breathed a sigh of relief. For a minute there, she'd thought another mini-war was about to be declared. But her roommates were in too good a mood. Toby felt another sharp pang of envy. Before this day is over, she thought as they entered the Dining Hall, I'm going to call Neal.

The weather didn't improve. A slate-colored sky hid the sun, and a trace of morning fog cast a chill over the carnival workers. Hands felt stiff as cardboard, faces were rubbed raw by the wind. The temptation to give up and seek warmer shelter tugged at all of them, but no one wanted to be the first to quit.

"We don't have that much time left," Andy reminded them as one particularly vicious gust of wind slapped their faces. She knew what everyone was thinking, and it made her nervous. They just couldn't afford to waste a whole day. "Besides," she added, "working will keep us warm."

Dee grunted. Dressed in an old blue sweatsuit, she was on her knees, hammering the final nail into the side of a booth. "I can think of lots of better ways to keep warm. Even vacuuming the halls doesn't seem so awful now. At least it's indoor work!"

"You've been spoiled by all that California sunshine," Cary pointed out as he checked the booth they'd just finished. "Spring in the East may be unpredictable, but it's more interesting than three hundred and sixty-five days of sunshine. Bor-ing."

"Don't be silly! We get rain in California. Haven't you ever heard about our mudslides? Have to have water to make mud, Cary, or didn't you get that far in science class yet?"

Before Cary could come up with a suitable reply, Maggie called out, "Hey, guys, we're getting company!" They all stopped what they were doing and looked up. A small group of adults in raingear was crossing the lawn, coming toward the work site. Through the faint drizzle that had begun to fall, Andy made out one familiar person. Standing up, hammer in hand, she said, "That's Leo."

"From the picket line?" Jane asked, frowning.

"Yes. And don't you say one unkind word, Jane Barrett, or I'll see that you get those horrid green sheets every single day from now on! At least give them a chance to tell us what they want."

Jane shrugged. "I wasn't going to say anything. Arguing in public is gauche. Everyone knows that."

As the group moved closer, it became clear that they were carrying cardboard cartons instead of cardboard picket signs. The cartons, they soon discovered happily when the adults arrived, contained styrofoam cups filled with steaming hot chocolate. There were big, fat sugar cookies, too.

"For us?" Andy cried with delight.

Leo nodded. His stocky frame was protected from the weather by an old navy blue raincoat and a floppy tweed hat. "We thought," he told Andy, extending the carton toward her, "that it was time to return your kindness to us. Seeing you out here, workin' away in this kind of weather, well, it seemed like the right time."

"Oh, Leo, this is so nice of you."

"Wasn't just me," he said, waving a hand toward the women with him. "Mamie here, she said shouldn't those young people have somethin' warm to heat up their bones?"

"Well, thank you, Mamie!" Andy said with warmth. "You'll all share with us, won't you?"

She began passing the carton around. "After all, it's just as cold for you as it is for us. And there's plenty here."

They all took a break then, milling around drinking the soothing hot chocolate, stamping cold feet to warm them, urging the adults to join them.

"Oh, no, that's all right. We've got to get back." Leo glanced around. "Looks like you're doin' real well here. Got quite a bit done already, haven't you? Have any trouble with that dunk tank? After I explained the plans, I mean?"

Remembering her wrestling match with the hose, Andy laughed. "Well, not really. We tested it and it seems to be working okay."

Another vicious gust of wind roared across campus, tugging at coats and hair and cups of hot chocolate.

"This really helps," Cary called to the small group of adults, holding up his cup. "Thanks a lot!" Others added their shouted thanks to his.

Leo flushed with pleasure. "No problem. Glad to help. Truth is, I guess we feel somewhat responsible. Weren't for the strike, we'd be doin' most of the carnival work."

"You've got *that* right," a cold, uncomfortable Jane said sharply.

"Jane!" Embarrassed, Andy turned back to Leo. "I'm sorry. She didn't mean that."

"I did so." Jane couldn't remember now why she hadn't gone home when her mother wanted her to. "Anyway, *he* said it first. I was just agreeing with him, that's all."

"Since when are you so agreeable?" Cary wanted to know. Replacing his empty cup in the cardboard carton, he faced Jane. "These people went out of their way to do a really nice thing for all of us. Why don't you just thank them?"

Jane glanced at him, her eyes flashing with anger. Her blonde hair, dampened by the drizzle, clung to her cheeks. "I am out in this miserable weather," she said, "because of these people. I appreciate the hot chocolate and cookies. We all do. But that doesn't mean that I think what they're doing is right." Turning to Leo, she said, "You've caused a lot of people a lot of trouble. This school could still close because of what you're doing and then where would you be? Isn't *any* job better than no job at all?"

"Jane, stop it!" Andy tugged at Jane's elbow. "Just cut it out."

Jane shook her hand away. "I have a right to say how I feel. You aren't the only one who has that right."

"I know," Andy pleaded. "But — "

There was a moment of awkward silence. Then Leo said to Andy, "We'd better go. We didn't come here to make trouble."

"I know that, Leo. And you didn't make trouble." She glared at Jane, who turned away, her back stiff and unyielding. "We *are* grateful. It was a really nice thing to do. Thanks."

Her companions called out their thanks, including Jane, who said with great dignity, "Yes, thank you. It was very nice of you."

The drizzle had turned into a light but steady rain. "Shouldn't you all go home?" Andy asked Leo as he turned to leave. "You're all going to get soaked."

"Oh, no. We stay on the picket line until dark. That's our rule and we'll stick by it." He laughed. "Don't worry, takes more than a little sour weather to stop us." His fellow strikers nodded agreement and they all left, trudging off into the curtain of rain until they disappeared from sight.

"I'll bet," Andy said almost to herself as raindrops slid down her cheeks, "they'd give anything to be safe and snug in a nice, warm house right now."

"Then why don't they go there?" Jane snapped. "They're not chained to that picket line. So what's stopping them?"

"A little thing called determination," Cary snapped back. "Ever heard of it?"

Toby had had enough. "Can you just please stop all this arguing?" she pleaded. "It's giving me a headache. We've got enough problems without fighting among ourselves."

"The girl has a point," Cary agreed. "Look, we can't get anything done in this weather. Might as well put away the tools and cover the lumber. If it's nice tomorrow, we'll just have to work twice as hard."

As anxious as Andy was to accomplish something, the thought of her nice, warm, dry room was too tempting to resist. She had a new book to read and the box of goodies that had accompanied the book, sent by her parents. Not a bad way to spend a rainy Sunday afternoon. If it weren't for the carnival work left undone, she'd relax and enjoy it.

Even though Jane knew what the answer would be, she asked Cary if he'd like to come in and visit in the lobby for a while. After all, they'd had a good time last night. And what had she said to the strikers that was so terrible, anyway? Just the truth. Cary believed in the truth, didn't he? He *said* he did.

But not this time, apparently. Because his response to her invitation was a cool, carefully phrased, "No, thank you." He said nothing about her remarks to Leo and the others. But, standing there in the rain watching him leave with Matt, she knew why he'd used that tone of voice. He didn't approve of her attitude about the strike.

And yet, look what it was doing to all of them. And to the school. If Cary Slade wanted to judge someone, why didn't he judge the people responsible for this mess? Why pick on her? *She* hadn't started it!

Soaking wet and shivering with cold, the Canby Hall girls put all of the tools away and hurried to their respective dorms to get dry and comfortable.

The minute Toby had changed into dry clothes and wrapped a towel around her wet hair, she hurried to the telephone to call Neal. Just the sound of his voice lifted her spirits. "You sound really beat, Toby. Bad day?"

"Well, it started out okay. But then the weather got really bad. And then the strikers brought us hot chocolate and cookies." She hesitated. How could she tell him what had happened. He'd been Jane's friend before she'd ever met him.

"That's a bad thing?" he asked, amusement in his voice. "What have you got against hot chocolate and cookies?"

"What? Oh, no, they were great. It's just that it started an argument about the strike, so it was kind of spoiled."

"Jane?"

"Excuse me?" She should have known he would guess. He knew Jane almost better than anyone.

"It was Jane, wasn't it? Your friends on the picket line did something nice for you and Jane just couldn't leave it alone, could she? She made some crack about everything being their fault in the first place. Am I right or am I right?"

He certainly did know Jane well. "They're not really my friends," Toby said, avoiding the questions about Jane. "It's Andy who's been really nice to them. They wanted to do something to pay her back, and they were nice enough to include all of us."

"And Jane spoiled it." His voice was flat. Toby wondered exactly how much it had hurt him when Jane turned to Cary. She hated the thought of Neal being in pain. He was so nice. Still, Jane couldn't help who she liked, could she?

And if she hadn't, a little voice inside her said, where would *you* be now? Certainly not talking to Cornelius Worthington III.

Out of gratitude to Jane for choosing Cary, Toby said loyally, "Well, she didn't *mean* to ruin things. But the weather was so nasty, we were all freezing, and we've been working like pack mules, so I know she was tired. I guess she just wasn't thinking."

"Yeah. Sometimes she forgets to do that," he said dryly. Toby wondered if he was thinking about that period when Jane had tried to balance both Cary and Neal in her life. Andy and Toby had disapproved and had told her so. But it had taken Jane a while to sort things out in her own mind and finally make an honest choice.

"You *are* coming up for the carnival, aren't you?" she asked him for what was probably the fiftieth time. "We're getting a lot done, even with no one to help us. We finally figured out the plans for the dunk tank. And it actually works! And we've built six booths so far. If the weather hadn't been so rotten today, we'd probably have finished more."

"You bet I'm coming. I wouldn't miss it. Besides," he added softly, "it gives me an excuse to see you."

"You don't need an excuse," Toby said honestly. "My goodness, if you only came up when we had a carnival, I'd only see you once a year."

"That's not enough?" he teased.

Toby was no game-player. She had never in her life batted an eyelash. "No, it's not," she said simply. "I don't think I'd like that at all."

"Me, either," Neal said, his voice serious. "I wouldn't like it at all."

By the time she crawled under her rainbow-striped comforter, Toby felt much better. It would be easier to sleep now. Thank goodness for Neal!

And Jane had shown only a friendly interest when Toby had returned to the room and told them she'd been talking with Neal — not a spark of jealousy, even though she and Cary weren't getting along.

They had skipped dinner because the room was too warm and cozy to leave and had instead eaten from Andy's goodie box. Then, sleepy from hard work and bad weather, Andy and Jane had fallen asleep.

Toby was sleepy, too. Glad that she had called Neal, happy that she'd be seeing him when it was carnival time, she rolled over and joined her roommates in sleep.

CHAPTER SEVENTEEN

The Canby Hall teachers had been supportive of the students' efforts by not assigning homework. But on Monday, the girls were told that things had to change. "We're getting behind in our work," their English teacher explained in her kind but firm voice. "You're here to be educated, not to learn how to put on a carnival or clean a dormitory. I'm sorry, girls, but your homework assignments will have to come first from now on."

"But, Ms. Eastman," Andy protested, "we're learning a lot of valuable things working on the carnival and cleaning the dorms. Shouldn't that count for something?"

"Yes, of course, Andrea. All learning counts for something. But you aren't being graded on the things you're doing and your teachers have no paperwork to show proof of your progress. Sooner or later, the Board of

Trustees will start asking questions, and we won't have any answers for them."

Andy made a face. There they were again, that mysterious Board of Trustees, messing everything up! A bunch of stuffy people sitting around a table somewhere making decisions that just made trouble for everyone. Why didn't they ever come on campus and talk to the people there? Maybe they'd learn something.

"Now, for tonight," the teacher said, "I want you to read . . ."

Andy tuned her out. She'd get the assignment later from someone. Right now, the situation at Canby Hall was on her mind. She probably wouldn't have time to do the homework, anyway.

The strike had gone on longer than she'd expected it to. Why did adults take so long to sort things out? How were they going to fit homework into a schedule already as tight as new shoes? She couldn't deny that they'd been coasting educationally. P.A. must have found out and put her foot down. Well, that was her job, wasn't it? Who could blame her?

I'll just have to stop sleeping, that's all, Andy told herself. Sleep is such a waste of time, anyway. So I get dark circles under my eyes, so I look like a raccoon, so what? I'll wear sunglasses. Forgetting for the moment that she was one of those people who fell instantly into profound unconsciousness every night, she nodded silently. Yep, that was it: She'd stop wasting precious hours making dents in her pillow. She'd just grab little naps whenever she could. And she'd ignore for now her dance teacher's constant reminder that "the human body needs plenty of rest, especially an active body."

The work session after school was plagued with problems. One of the boys from Ambulance accidentally split one sheet of lumber, ruining it.

Jane and Cary weren't speaking. They ignored each other. When they were forced to speak, they were excessively polite: "May I please have those nails, Jane?" "Certainly, Cary."

And the weather hadn't improved much. It wasn't as chilly as it had been, and the drizzle had ended. But the sky was charcoal gray, a sure sign of heavy rain to come. "We'd better cover the lumber when we finish today," Matt told Andy. "Rain won't hurt the finished booths, but I don't like working with wet lumber."

"That's all we need," Andy said in a cranky voice. "Rain! As if we didn't have enough problems already. Why doesn't somebody invent a longer day? Twenty-four hours just isn't enough."

"More time wouldn't help," he said, sounding very adult. "It would just fill up with more stuff, you know that."

"Yeah, I guess. But," she added wearily,

"whoever designed a twenty-four-hour day didn't have a carnival to put on, with employees on strike, and an English paper to write."

She turned to finish nailing a "BALLOON TOSS" sign on a booth and saw Merrie come out of Baker House and stride purposefully toward them. "Oh-oh! Something's up. Merrie's in a hurry and she doesn't look all that happy."

She wasn't. "We've got a major plumbing leak in the laundry room," she told them. "But I think we can fix it ourselves if someone will dash into the village and get me a few do-it-yourself supplies."

"No problem," Cary volunteered. Laying his saw aside, he stood up.

"Oh, thanks, Cary. You'll have to take one of the Canby girls with you. I have to use a voucher and the hardware store proprietor might not accept it from you." She smiled. "He'll know you're not a student here."

Jane stood up and wiped her hands on her jeans, prepared to be driven into town. She welcomed the chance to get away, even for a short while, and the drive would give her and Cary a chance to talk. Maybe this was the perfect opportunity to straighten things out. The plumbing leak was a lucky break for her.

Cary said, "Toby? Feel like a ride into town?"

Jane froze in place. Andy couldn't bear the look on her face. There was shock and anger and humiliation all blended together into one wide-eyed, pale-faced stare. Had he actually asked Toby to go along and not Jane?

Oblivious to what was going on around her, Merrie said casually, "Oh, that's a good idea. Toby, you run along. Here's the voucher." Handing it to her and seeing Toby's hesitation, she added, "Oh, go on, now. They can manage here without you for a little while. Hurry up, before Baker House is completely flooded out."

Toby really was torn. If she went with Cary, she'd be inviting Jane's anger which, as Toby well knew, was no small thing. But if she refused, she'd be calling merciless attention to Jane's misery. Cary obviously didn't want Jane along. He would have asked her in the first place. And he wouldn't have made a point of asking someone else. Even if I refuse now, Toby thought with clarity, he still won't ask Jane.

"Okay," she told Merrie quietly, "what do I need to get at the hardware store?" Merrie told her, and Toby followed Cary to his car. She never looked at Jane. She couldn't.

As Cary's car pulled away and Meredith left, everyone began talking fast, in loud voices, to prove that they weren't paying the slightest attention to Jane. She stood, stunned, her cheeks now flame-red, alone in the center of a great deal of sudden activity. Hoping to avoid a blow-up, Andy walked over to her.

"Jane, can you help me with these signs?" she asked as casually as she could manage. She really wanted to put her arms around her roommate and comfort her, but instinct told her that would be the worst possible move.

"What just happened here?" Jane asked in a bewildered voice.

"Jane, come on." Andy reached out to lay a hand on Jane's arm.

The arm was wrenched away. "No! Don't make me calm down! I'm angry and unless I'm crazy, I have every right to be angry. You saw what he just did. If Matt had done that to you, I wouldn't expect *you* to be calm."

But Matt wouldn't have done it, Andy thought. Sometimes Cary behaved every bit as much like a spoiled four-year-old as he accused Jane of being.

"This is," Jane declared, "just about the worst day of my life!"

"You said that last month when they served creamed spinach for dinner," Andy reminded her gently. "And you said it when Neal showed up on campus before you'd had a chance to tell him about Cary." Jane's eyes flashed angrily at the sound of his name. "And I think," Andy went on, "that you even said it yesterday."

"Hey, you guys," Dee called, "are you going to help or what? Quit standing around like statues."

Grateful for the interruption, Andy nodded. "Be right there." To Jane, she said, "C'mon, Jane, ease up. It's no big deal. It's not as if he took Toby to the theater in Boston. He just drove her to the hardware store." She grinned. "The *hardware store*, for Pete's sake!"

Jane unclenched her jaw.

"And they did it for Merrie. And for Baker House. So that's the same thing as doing it for all of us, right, Jane?"

Jane's color began returning to normal.

"Besides," Andy concluded, "I can't quite see you in a hardware store!"

Jane smiled. It was weak, like that of someone recovering from a long illness, but it was enough to allow Andy to relax a little. "Good!" she cried with relief, "Great! Now let's get back to work. It's almost time to quit for the day."

Another crisis over, she thought as they picked up their hammers. Now Jane won't pack her bags and head for Boston tonight. Maybe we'll get really lucky, and she'll actually speak to Cary and Toby again one day. Maybe even in this lifetime. If not, well . . . Andy shrugged. One could only do so much to keep the peace. She'd done her part. The rest was up to Jane and Toby and Cary. She, Andy, had a booth to finish.

Jane did speak to Toby again, probably because Cary and Toby were only gone long enough to drive to town and back and fit in a hurried five-minute visit to the hardware store. "See?" Andy whispered to Jane as Cary's car pulled up in front of Baker House, "I told you, it was strictly business. They obviously didn't elope, after all."

Jane managed a small laugh. And when Toby joined them, Jane was friendly enough, greeting her roommate as if nothing unusual had happened. She did not, however, extend the same courtesy to Cary. Whatever the reason, he had deliberately ignored her, in front of everyone. Maybe he was used to treating those girls who made such a fuss over Ambulance, screaming and jumping up and down and shouting Cary's name whenever the band played in town, that way. So juvenile. One smile from rude Cary Slade and they were ready to fall down on the floor in a dead faint.

Well, she wasn't one of them. She was practically an adult, and she was a Barrett. Cary Slade was not going to have a chance to trample on her self-respect again!

She noticed as she glanced at her watch that it was very late. They just had time to clean up their mess, cover the lumber, put the tools away, and get to the Dining Hall. Room 407 had kitchen duty tonight.

She made a point of telling every single member of the work crew good-bye except Cary. "Good-bye, Matt," "Good-bye, Doug," "Good-bye, Dennis," but no "Good-bye, Cary." He didn't deserve it.

But she accidentally caught his eye before she turned away, and the look on his face surprised her. He looked . . . sorry? Like he wanted to apologize?

Well, it was too late. Hardening her heart, she tipped her chin high in the air and whirled away from him. She didn't look back once as she made her way to the Dining Hall, flanked on either side by Toby and Andy, while Dee and Maggie helped the boys return the tools to their proper place in the basement of Baker House.

In the Dining Hall, someone at their table mentioned the pie-baking contest, a traditional part of the Almost Summer Carnival. When the pies had been tasted and judged, any remaining slices were sold, adding to the carnival profits. The girls of Room 407 had been told that the contest was a popular part of the carnival, and the tradition should be continued. Jane had forgotten all about it, probably because that was exactly what she'd wanted to do: forget about it.

"Well, I don't know about anyone else at this table," Jane announced, "but I put that useless contest right out of my head the minute I heard about it."

"Oh, Jane," Andy said with a grin, "I signed up for you. You can't go through your whole life without making at least one pie."

Jane stared at her. "Why do I need to learn how to make a pie when I can just go to the store and buy one? Besides," she added resolutely, "I am not the sort of person who should be covered with flour from head to toe."

"If you've never made a pie before," Maggie asked innocently, "how do you know flour is what you'd be covered with? Who told you so?"

Jane looked doubtful. "Isn't it? Isn't it flour?"

Maggie nodded. "Sure. I just wondered how you knew."

"I guess I saw it on television. Or maybe my mother baked one once."

The image of the elegant Mrs. Barrett in a kitchen, probably in an apron, up to her elbows in flour, was too much for Andy and Toby. They dissolved into contagious giggles, and soon everyone at the table, most of whom had seen Jane's mother at least once, was laughing, too, including Jane.

On the way back to the dorm after their clean-up chores, Toby said suddenly, "On the trip into town, Jane, all Cary talked about was you."

"That must have been interesting," Jane remarked after a moment or two. "Fifteen minutes of heated discussion about the spoiled rich girl."

"Um-um." Toby shook her head. "He said you were very special." She grinned. "And he said . . . he said," she ran laughing up the steps of Baker House, "he said you drive him nuts!"

CHAPTER EIGHTEEN

Jane hurried to the work site after classes the following day convinced that Cary was ready to make up. Hadn't Toby said that Cary had talked about her during their trip into town? So how mad could he really be? It wouldn't kill *her* to apologize, either, she thought as she strode across campus in jeans and a Canby Hall T-shirt.

I *will* apologize, she decided. Feeling very generous about the whole thing, she reached the work site and approached an already-busy Cary.

"Hi!" she called brightly, touching his shoulder. "Got a minute to talk?" Everyone else was too busy to pay any attention to them, although Jane did notice Toby glancing over as Jane arrived.

"No." The answer was curt. It left little room for doubt.

"Cary, come on," she probed softly. "That

booth isn't going to run away. You can take a couple of minutes. I want to tell you something."

He twisted his head to look up at her. She knew that look, and all of her optimism dissolved like sugar in hot coffee. It was the look he wore whenever he decided that their relationship was a big mistake.

"Sorry, no can do," he said, turning back to his booth. "We're behind schedule as is. No time for gossip."

Gossip? Could he actually believe she just wanted to gossip? Since when was she someone who spread tales about other people? He knew better than that.

For just a second, Jane was strongly tempted to plunk herself down on the grass beside Cary and *make* him listen to her. She'd tug on his single earring or pull at his hair if that was what it took. Anything to get their relationship back to normal.

But Jane's pride had the strength of ten strong people. It kept her standing upright and stiffened her resolve against begging. She had tried, hadn't she? She had made a great effort to apologize, and Cary had refused to listen. Well, she could be every bit as stubborn as Cary Slade. Elephants would fly before she'd try apologizing to *him* again.

As she moved away from him, she felt Toby's eyes on her. Mind your own business, she wanted to say. But she had enough problems. She didn't need to make Toby mad, too. So she said nothing, going straight to work instead.

During the afternoon, whenever she glanced angrily in Cary's direction, he was either concentrating totally on his work or laughing at someone's joke. As far as Jane knew, he never looked her way.

Andy held a nail while Matt hammered it in. "Boy, I wish I knew what was going on with Jane and Cary," she said quietly. "They aren't even talking to each other."

"Oh, you know them." He gave the nail one final blow. "They're always on the outs. And they always make up. Quit worrying."

She handed him another nail. "I know, but I hate it when Jane's mad at Cary. She takes it out on everyone around her. And who's around her more than Toby and me?"

Matt pounded away before answering, as if hammering at the nail might provide him with an answer. "Why don't you just ignore her? That's what Cary's doing."

"But that's exactly why she's mad! It's not fair to Jane. And I don't want her mad at me. We've got enough problems right now without the occupants of Room 407 in Baker House not speaking to each other. We're already walking on eggs because of our differences about the strike. I try not to mention it, and so does Toby. I guess Jane does, too, now that I think about it."

Matt bent to pick up a saw. "Well, this is

really Jane's problem," he said, "not yours. Whatever's going on between her and Cary is for them to fix, right?"

Andy knew he was right. But it was so frustrating, watching Jane work in silent misery while Cary ignored her.

But Andy's sympathy began to dissipate rapidly during a meal of hot vegetable soup and hero sandwiches in the Dining Hall that evening, as Jane kept up a steady stream of complaints. She began with the meal: the soup was too cold, the sandwich too bulky, how could anyone possibly put such a monstrosity into one's mouth, and didn't the milk taste a little sour? Then she complained about the state of the Dining Hall, insisting that someone wasn't doing her chores properly because that was definitely a gum wrapper on the floor over there, and certainly no one had had chewing gum for dinner, so the wrapper had probably been there for hours, maybe even days.

"Jane," Andy said patiently, remembering that Jane was probably still stinging from Cary's treatment of her, "*we* cleaned in here last night and we did *not* leave any gum wrappers on the floor. Someone probably just dropped it."

Shaking her head at the thought of such carelessness, Jane searched for something else to complain about, and found it. Why, she wondered aloud, did they have to put all of the tools away each and every day when they

were just going to use them again the following afternoon? It made no sense.

"Because," Toby said, "it's spring now and
everybody tells me the weather is really weird
here in the springtime and it could rain at
any time. If we ruined the tools by leaving
them out in the rain, we'd be in real trouble.
Anyway," she added lightly, "it's no big deal
to put them back in the basement, is it, Jane?
I mean, we have to go back to Baker House to
wash up for dinner, anyway. Might as well
carry the tools with us."

"Well, I think it's stupid," Jane insisted.

Andy noticed that she hadn't touched her
dinner. Oh, dear. A starving person would
be a cranky person. "Jane, eat your dinner,"
she ordered mildly.

"I'm not hungry. Not for this stuff. I want
a *real* meal. I want mashed potatoes and thick
slices of roast beef and steamed vegetables
and . . ."

"Stop it, Jane!" Andy ordered, not so mildly
this time. "The food sitting in front of you is
better than we're used to, and you know it.
You're just in a bad mood and ready to complain about every single thing you can think
of. Just cut it out."

Jane clamped her lips together. She didn't
say another word throughout the meal or on
the walk back to Baker House.

They sat in Room 407 in gloomy silence,
pretending to study. But Jane kept rapping

her pencil against her endtable, which made concentration impossible. "Jane," Toby finally cried in exasperation, "why don't you go take a shower? It will relax you. And *that* will *relax* us!"

"I'm not ready to take a shower," Jane said loftily, her eyes on the notebook on her lap.

"Well, then, I'm going to. Anything to get out of this room!" And Toby gathered together her shampoo and robe and left, rolling her eyes in sympathy for Andy as she went out the door.

A few silent minutes later, someone knocked on the door. A voice called, "Telephone call for October Houston. Long-distance. The room phone lines aren't working, so the calls are coming in downstairs."

"Tell them to call back," Andy called quickly, but just as quickly, Jane jumped out of bed and cried, "No, wait! I'll take it."

"Jane, you can't take Toby's phone call."

"It's okay. I'm sure it's Neal. I'll just keep him busy until Toby's through in the shower." Glancing over her shoulder as she opened the door, Jane grinned and said, "Don't forget, Andy, Neal and I were friends long before Toby even knew there *was* a Massachusetts. We always have lots to talk about." And she was gone, leaving Andy staring after her, stern disapproval on her face.

Running down the hall, Jane felt light and happy. Of course! Neal was the perfect person to talk to. She would have called him herself, but she'd been afraid he'd report her complaints to her parents, who would then come up and drag her out of school. Even now, she'd have to be a little careful about what she said to Neal, but she could still talk to him.

"Hi, Neal," she said breezily, picking up the phone. "It's Jane. Toby's in the shower, so you're stuck with me. How are you?"

When he asked her the same question, she told him. She told him about the strike, although she was careful to reassure him that they were handling things just fine, thank you very much. No problem. (She had to cross her fingers behind her back on that one.) Then she told him about Andy's high-handed attitude about the strikers, giving him no chance to agree or disagree with her opinion of Andy's position. And, finally, she told him about Cary. "He's the most stubborn, pigheaded person I've ever met, Neal," she said earnestly. "I mean, I know I'm not always right. How could I be? But there I was, perfectly willing to apologize, and he wouldn't even listen. Is that fair?"

Neal Worthington probably knew Jane Barrett better than anyone else at Canby Hall. At one time, not so very long ago, their parents had expected them to marry one day. Then Jane had met Cary and Neal had met Toby, and that was that. Neal had wished Cary luck at the time, and he still did. Jane could be the sweetest person in the world. She could also be one of the most demanding.

And he did *not* want to get involved in this. Jane was still his friend, true. But this business with Cary was something she should take to her boyfriend, not him. "Look, about the strike," he said, choosing a safer topic, "Andy probably just wants to help get things straightened out. You know how she is when people are down. She'll bend over backwards if she has to, to help them get back up."

He was taking Andy's side? Hadn't he heard a word she'd said?

"Just try seeing things from the strikers' point of view," he said, bringing her blood to a slow boil. "They probably don't have it all that easy, Jane. If they did, they wouldn't have walked off the job in the first place."

Jane stood silently for several moments. If there was one thing she was sick of, it was being talked to as if she were a two-year-old child. And from Neal, of all people! Who did he think he was? He didn't know any more about how working-class people lived or worked than she did.

"Neal," she said simply, "I'm going to hang up now." And she did. She was back in her room, sitting on her bed, her face a dark cloud of anger when Toby came in, a white towel wrapped around her head.

"You had a phone call," Andy said quickly, glancing at Jane with a question in her eyes. "Jane took it." She didn't want any trouble, but Toby had a right to know that Neal had called, and Andy wasn't at all sure that Jane planned to tell her.

"Oh?" Toby looked at Jane. "Was it Neal? Did he say he'd call back?"

Jane shook her head. "No, he didn't say anything about calling back." She didn't look up, and she didn't add that she hadn't given Neal a chance to mention calling back.

"You were out there in the hall quite a while," Andy said slowly to Jane. "Were you talking to Neal all that time?"

Jane didn't answer.

"Why didn't you come and get me?" Toby asked, walking over to sit down on her bed. "I could have grabbed a robe. I hate missing Neal's calls; you know that. What did you talk to him about? And why didn't you keep him on the line for me?"

Jane shook her head. "We didn't talk about anything special." She looked at Toby. "I just thought since Neal and I are friends, you wouldn't mind if I talked to him." She fixed her eyes on Toby's. "You don't mind, do you?"

Toby wasn't sure. She was remembering that Jane and Neal had been more than just friends, and that Jane and Cary weren't speaking to each other.

"Anyway," Jane added hastily, "you don't need to mind, because it was a stupid conversation. Neal just isn't as sensitive as he used to be. He's changed."

"That means," Andy said dryly, "that you complained about the strike and he didn't sympathize with you."

Ignoring Andy's remark, Jane addressed Toby. "You're tired of all this hard work, too, I know you are. Just don't complain about it to Neal, because he'll just give you a lecture. He didn't even care that I have blisters . . . blisters! on my hands."

Toby laughed. "Oh, Jane," she said, "I wouldn't complain to Neal about the strike in the first place. Because now that I've seen for myself what it takes to keep this place running, I understand why the workers went out on strike. I don't blame them a bit. And I already explained all of that to Neal, so he knows how I feel. And he feels the same way."

Jane's cheeks flushed a brilliant red. Furious, and feeling betrayed by just about everyone she knew, she slid under her blankets and flopped over on her side, away from her roommates.

By concentrating very hard, she was able to hold back angry tears and, eventually, fall asleep.

CHAPTER NINETEEN

Jane awoke to a shattering noise on Saturday morning. It sounded like a thousand high-heeled tap dancers cavorting on the roof of Baker House. She was a reluctant riser under the best of circumstances, and the deafening clatter that assaulted her ears sent her burrowing deeper beneath her blankets.

"What is that awful racket?" she cried from her snug little burrow.

"Hail," Andy called from her bed. "It's hail. The temperature's gone into the cellar and the wind has gone crazy, and it's hailing like mad."

Jane cautiously raised her head. And heard, above the hail's rat-a-tat-tat, the wind screaming around the building. Shivering at the mournful sound, she slid back down, pulling her comforter up around her ears. "What time is it?" she called. Not that she had any intention of going out in such miserable weather.

"It's seven-fifteen in the A.M.," Andy replied. "But I only know that because I have a watch. The alarm didn't go off because the electricity *did*. Go off, I mean. I guess the wind blew down the lines."

Jane groaned. No electricity? She ticked off in her head the different ways that would affect her life on this Saturday: no blow-dryer, no electric rollers, no light so she could see herself in a mirror . . . and maybe, horror of horrors, no hot water. Did the hot water heater run on electricity? She wasn't sure.

Andy got up, wrapping a blanket around her shoulders, and went to the window.

"Don't get too close to it," Toby cautioned. "We've had hail at home, some of it big as baseballs, and it can shatter every window in a house. Cut you to ribbons if you get too close."

Andy jumped backward and sat down on her bed. "Whew!" she said suddenly, dropping the blanket, "isn't it awfully warm in here? I know it's cold outside because I had the window open before you guys woke up. It wasn't hailing then, just blowing like crazy, and I wanted to check out the storm. But it was so cold out there, I shut the window right away. So why is it like a sauna in here?"

"Maybe someone turned on the furnace," Toby suggested as Jane sat up in bed, rubbing her eyes.

Andy shook her head doubtfully. "Well,

maybe, but if they did, the thermostats have gone crazy. It's never this hot in here."

"Never mind that," Jane said impatiently. "What about this storm? Don't you realize it's probably destroying all of our hard work on the carnival? Listen to that wind howling! The booths we tossed together won't be able to stand up to that."

Toby and Andy stared at each other in dismay. The sound of glass breaking somewhere in the distance startled them, fortifying their concern. There was muted shouting then, followed by more shattering glass. And in the next instant, their own window, under attack by golf-ball-sized spheres of ice, splintered into a thousand pieces, showering the desk area with chunks and slivers of glass. The wind whooshed into the room with a roar.

The girls screamed and ran to the door as the wind tore at their hair and clothes.

"Out!" Andy urged, gasping for breath, "let's get out of here!" Jane tugged on the doorknob, but the howling wind slammed against the door so hard it shook in its frame. There was no budging it. Hail hammered against the desk, the lamp, the floor, with sharp rattling sounds. "Hurry," Andy urged, "hurry *up!*"

"I can't," Jane gasped, "I can't get the door open. *Help* me!" She grabbed the knob with both hands, Andy clutched Jane around the waist, and Toby held Andy the same way, and all three pulled. When Jane managed to get the door open by an inch or so, she used her foot to thrust a book into the space to keep the door from being blown shut again.

"Pull harder!" she shouted above the wind and hail. And when Toby and Andy obeyed, the door yielded, and they were flung out into the safety of the hall. Behind them, another gust of wind slammed the door shut.

The hall was full of frightened girls in pajamas and robes, talking about broken windows and glass everywhere and the awful sounds of the storm. Merrie, in a long red robe, her hair loose around her shoulders, was trying to calm everyone down. "There are no windows in this hall," she reminded them, "so you're perfectly safe." And then added as if talking to herself, "*Why* is it so hot in here?" She passed through the group, touching a shoulder, patting a hand. Then, reaching the girls from 407, looked down and said, "Toby. You're bleeding. You've cut your foot."

Startled, all three girls looked down at Toby's bare feet. One of them had a neat, even slash down its side.

"You'll never get to the infirmary in this storm," Merrie said as Toby stared down at her wounded foot. "Come into the bathroom and I'll wrap that foot in a clean towel." Looking up, she called, "Is anyone else hurt? Any cuts or bruises?" No one stepped forward. Merrie turned back to Toby. "Okay, good. Come on, Toby. Everyone else wait

right here. Do *not* go back into your rooms.
I'll be right back." Toby followed Merrie
down the hall, leaving a thin trail of blood
behind her as she walked. They disappeared
into the bathroom.

Andy watched them go. Only her pride
kept her from bursting into tears. It wasn't
fear of the storm that upset her. It was what the
storm had to be doing to all their hard work
that was sending her into a tailspin. The dunk
tank was full of water and wouldn't be going
anywhere, too heavy for even a wind such as
this one to move. But the booths wouldn't be
so lucky. She could picture the nails pulling
away from the lumber, the carefully sawed
boards flying about campus, scattering this
way and that like Tinkertoys.

The rattle of the hail stopped. They all fell
silent to listen. Had it really ended, that
nerve-wracking, machine-gun staccato on the
roof and windows?

It had. It was replaced by a heavy drum-
ming sound.

"It's pouring," Merrie announced as she
and Toby, foot awkwardly wrapped in a thick
white towel, rejoined the group in the hall.
"Coming down in buckets! I could hear it in
the bathroom. But at least the hail has
stopped."

Enormous relief set them all talking at
once, chattering about who had had the most
damage, who had been in the worst peril.

"Girls, please!" Merrie cried, waving her

arms to get their attention. "Didn't you hear me say it was pouring? Those of you whose windows were shattered are going to return to a river in your room if we don't do something. We'll have to tack blankets across the window and hope that will keep some of the rain out. *After* we carefully clean up all of the broken glass, of course." She began issuing directions, "Dee, you and Maggie get me some nails and a hammer. Carol, you and Teresa bring a couple of vacuum cleaners. Get extra ones from the other floors. We'll need those for the smallest bits of glass. And will someone *please* check out the furnace in the basement. It's like a tropical jungle in here!"

"We don't know anything about furnaces," Jane protested. "What good would it do for one of us to check it out?"

"All you have to do," her housemother explained, "is shut off the gas valve. That will do the trick for now. Without gas, the furnace can't operate. There's a little valve on the bottom on the left. It's painted bright red. It looks like a faucet, and you can't miss it. Just turn it off."

That seemed simple enough. "I'll go," Jane volunteered.

"Well, take someone with you. And be careful," glancing up toward the roof and the sound of heavy rain, "there may be water in the basement already. It leaks, and that rain has been coming down hard."

Then she turned back to the group of girls

milling about her in the hall. "Girls, we're not going to get out to the Dining Hall for breakfast or lunch, and possibly not for dinner, either." Everyone groaned. "Well, some of you can hunt up any food available right here in Baker House. Everyone's care packages will have to become community property today."

No one noticed that Jane went alone to the stairs. She saw no need to take someone with her. Merrie was going to need all the help she could get in cleaning up the rooms and covering the windows. And it only took one person to turn off a gas valve, didn't it? She hurried down the stairs, wiping perspiration from her forehead as she went.

On the fourth floor, Merrie and her charges quickly discovered that covering large windows with blankets in the face of a fierce wind and sheets of slanting rain was no small task.

"At least it's cooler in here than it is in the hall," Merrie said lightly as they wrestled with the corners of a wind-whipped gray wool blanket. "I guess there are *some* advantages to having a broken window. It lets the cool breeze in." She was hoping to get even a small smile from her six helpers. None came. They were too intent on their battle to tack down the edges of the blanket without falling out of the fourth-floor window. They would capture one blanket corner only to lose another to the wind. And keeping their balance so close to a large, open window was not easy with the wind swirling around them, tugging at them, blowing their hair in their eyes.

"This is impossible!" a girl named Karen shouted, her face wet with rain, her long, dark hair tangled around her face. "The blanket's already soaked! What good is it going to do even if we get it tacked up?"

"It's just better than nothing," Merrie gasped as she triumphantly imprisoned one corner. "There! Now let's get the other corners fastened down. We have other rooms to do."

Although she was careful not to show her real feelings, Meredith did not like this nasty storm one little bit. She was accustomed to erratic weather during an eastern spring, but she couldn't remember many as vicious as this one. It had already done so much damage.

"Okay, we did it!" Meredith said cheerfully. Swiping at her wet face and hair with the sleeve of her red robe, she urged her helpers onward. "Let's go. We've got more windows to cover."

When they moved out into the hall, it seemed cooler. "Good!" Merrie exclaimed with relief, "Jane must have found the gas valve on the furnace." She glanced up and down the hall. It was busy with girls carrying mops or vacuum cleaners or wastebaskets full of broken glass. But there was no sign of Jane. "I wonder where she is," Merrie murmured. "Well, she's around somewhere. Probably cleaning up after her trip to the basement.

C'mon, let's check out Room 401. Somebody said it had one of the broken windows."

Where Jane was, was in the basement. Still in pajamas, robe and the slippers she automatically slid into any time she got out of bed, she had realized almost immediately upon entering the basement that she should have brought a flashlight with her. This was an old basement, the sort that Stephen King would write about, Jane thought. It was dark and damp and probably full of spiders. Had it been night, it would have been too dark to see anything. Even daylight on this dark, stormy day didn't help much. But the faint light coming in through the high windows allowed her to see that Meredith had been right about the basement leaking: at least an inch of water covered the floor.

Jane hesitated on the bottom step. No point in ruining a perfectly good pair of slippers. She slid out of them and bent to roll up her pajama legs and hitch her long pink bathrobe up to her hips, where she tied the edges into a loose knot. Thus clad, she took a deep breath and stepped into the water swirling across the basement floor. It was very cold, and she gasped in shock.

"Now," she muttered as she began wading, "if I were a furnace valve, where would I be?"

CHAPTER TWENTY

Upstairs, Meredith and her assistants went from room to room, from floor to floor. They cleaned up broken glass and tacked blankets to window frames wherever it was necessary. The wind had eased up a little, making part of their task less of a challenge. But the rain continued to pound down upon Baker House in what seemed to Andy an attempt to drive the building straight into the ground.

"Can you imagine what this is doing to our poor booths?" she moaned, sweeping up pieces of glass with a broom and dustpan. "They're probably nothing more than matchsticks now," she added mournfully. "Just tiny little pieces of splintered wood decorating the campus. And all the king's horses and all the king's men won't be able to put our booths back together again."

"Oh, Andy," Dee snapped, dumping broken

glass into a wastebasket, "must you be so cheerful?"

"Sorry." It wasn't like her to be so pessimistic. But waking up this morning to the sound of their carnival being blown to the four corners of the earth had dealt her natural optimism a severe blow. "Maybe the booths will be okay. I mean, we really gave those nails a good pounding. And Leo said we'd done a good job." Her voice lacked conviction and she knew it. But she just couldn't shake the sickening feeling that this awful storm was grinding all of their hard work into sawdust.

At least the temperature in the building had cooled. "Where *is* Jane, anyway?" Andy asked irritably. "How long does it take to turn off one little valve? We need her up here."

It wasn't the valve that was giving Jane trouble in the basement. Pink robe hitched up around her hips, pajama legs rolled to the knee, she had waded through the icy water to the furnace and found the valve. When she crouched and turned it off, the furnace gave a little whoosh and died. So much for that, Jane thought with satisfaction. Then, as she stood up, ankle-deep in water, her eye caught movement off to her left. Turning her head, she understood exactly *why* she was ankle-deep in water. There was a hole in the basement's stone wall, through which water was pouring at an alarming rate. And the rainstorm outside continued unabated.

"Oh, for Pete's sake!" Jane cried, "wasn't

the furnace enough!" She stood with hands on hips, peering through the basement's gloom. That hole had to be plugged, even though she couldn't do anything about the water already tugging at her feet. But there must be something she could do about that gaping cylindrical hole in the wall.

"Well, Jane," she said aloud, "what is it that people do to a hole when they don't want the hole? They plug it up, don't they?"

The water pouring into the basement gushed and gurgled in reply.

Jane continued to peer about the basement. It was an old-fashioned cellar, full of boxes and trunks and tools. There had to be something in all that junk that would serve as a plug. Just as she thought this, Jane spotted what looked like a pile of logs, not far from where the water was gushing in. Wading over to it, she discovered that it was indeed a pile of logs in all shapes and sizes, probably for use in Merrie's fireplace and in the fireplace in the front parlor. The wood was wet. No one would be starting any fires with it for a while. But one of the logs might be just what she needed.

After a long five minutes she found one just the right size. She slopped back and forth through the water from the hole to the log pile and back again, carrying one log each time. Two were too big. Two were too small, but encouraged her in her quest for the proper size because she could see that she had the right idea. After the very first try, her clothes were saturated and sticking to her. Her hands were wet and so cold they hurt when she picked up a log. Because it was almost impossible to work with stiff hands, she sloshed back to the stairs and slid one hand into each of the slippers she'd left there. They were warm and furry and provided instant relief. And the bottoms, now covering the palms of her hands, were leather and would provide a better grip on the logs. Grinning at both her own ingenuity and the sight of her hands encased in pink fur, a sodden Jane returned to the log pile.

When she found exactly the right plug and had jammed it into the hole, stopping the flow of water, Jane shouted, "Hooray!" at the top of her lungs. "I did it!" she yelled happily, "how about that?" She felt great, in spite of the fact that every inch of her was cold and wet. She had done what Merrie asked her to and then some. Now she was more than ready to go back upstairs, to get dried off and into warm, dry clothes, and relax. She shivered and shuffled through the water to the stairs. The climb upward with water adding extra weight to her clothes and hair was very tiring, and Jane reached for the doorknob with relief. She turned it and pushed.

Nothing happened.

She pushed again, harder this time. Still nothing. The door, an old wooden one, wasn't budging in its frame.

"Oh, come on," Jane moaned, "don't do this to me! I'm cold and I'm soaked and I'm tired and I want out of this stupid basement!"

But the door ignored her plea. And when she quit pushing and struggling and began pounding on it and yelling for help, the only reply she got was the echo of her own voice. Where *was* everybody? Why didn't someone come and rescue her? Exhausted, Jane sagged against the basement wall, shaking her head wearily.

No one came to her rescue because everyone was busy in other parts of the building. Jane's voice was easily drowned out by the banging of hammers against nails and the rain pounding down on Baker House.

"I am *not*," Jane told the immovable door, "going to stand here all day freezing!" There was, she knew, a small door in the basement that led directly outside. They had used it several times when returning the tools. Going outside in this weather would be as unpleasant as wading through that cold water again, but what choice did she have? Besides, she thought as she turned and descended the stairs again, I'm already soaked. Wet, wetter, wettest, what's the difference?

She had discarded the sodden slippers permanently after plugging up the hole, and the icy water chilled her feet as she left the bottom step. The little door, she remembered, was at the end of a narrow corridor reached by climbing a set of stone steps. Feeling a little like the heroine in an adventure movie, Jane took a step forward. But she was unable to take a second step, because something had wound itself around her right ankle and was holding it in a viselike grip. Her leg might as well have been shackled to the stone floor. Although she pulled and tugged, the ankle was held fast. "Now what?" Jane groaned, looking down.

At first she thought what she saw beneath the dark water was a snake. One hand went to her mouth in horror, stifling a scream. Then two things changed her mind: a basic knowledge of science that told her snakes do not have brass nozzles, and the realization that Baker House didn't allow pets.

"It's a garden hose," she told the furnace. "A perfectly harmless garden hose."

Still, if it was harmless, she wondered, why was it giving her so much trouble? And who had hidden this stupid hose under the water in the first place? Andy. Hadn't she and Matt had the hose the other day? They obviously hadn't returned it to its rack on the wall where it belonged. And then the water had poured in through the wall, hiding the hose from sight. She'd been lucky enough to avoid it because she'd gone straight to the furnace the first time she'd entered the basement. But this time, she'd turned left. I'll get Andy, Jane thought fiercely — if I ever get out of here. She bent to untangle her captured foot.

* * *

Upstairs, Andy and Toby had changed into jeans and sweatshirts and were cleaning up the last of the glass on the first floor when they heard pounding on the front door. "That doesn't sound like a storm noise," Toby said, cocking her head to one side. "I think someone wants in."

"Don't be ridiculous! Who'd be out in this weather?" But Andy listened, too. The knocking came again, more insistent this time.

"Someone *is* out there!" Andy ran downstairs to pull the heavy door open. Matt and Cary, enveloped in yellow rubber raingear, stood before her, their faces dripping wet, gasping, "What on earth took you so long?" They stumbled inside, shaking water around them like puppies.

"Why were you out in this?" Andy asked, taking their raincoats from them and hanging them on the huge old wooden coat rack in the hall.

"Coming to your rescue," Matt answered with a grin. He brushed wet hair away from his forehead. "We had a few broken windows from the hail, so we figured you probably did, too. Our maintenance people are fixing ours. Since you don't *have* any maintenance people right now, we thought you might be able to use some help."

"We did it ourselves," Andy declared proudly.

"You fixed broken windows?"

"Well . . . we didn't really fix them. I mean, we just covered them with blankets. But it helps a little."

"Not a bad idea," Cary said. "Isn't this weather wild? The hail was bad enough but all this rain! I've never seen it come down so hard. There'll be flooding on campus, take my word for it. And I'll bet our carnival stuff is really taking a beating." He glanced around the hall. "Where's Jane?" Although he wasn't quite ready to admit it to Jane, he'd been worried about her. And worrying about her had convinced him that they were silly to keep having these dumb arguments about the strike. What did it have to do with them, anyway?

Andy searched the hall with her eyes as if she expected Jane to pop out from behind the coat rack or the door to the library. "Gosh, I don't know. Merrie sent her downstairs to fix the furnace, but that was a long time ago. Maybe she went back to our room."

Cary laughed. "Jane? Was supposed to fix a furnace? You're kidding, right?"

Doubt slid across Andy's face. "All she had to do was turn off a little valve." Glancing down at her watch, she said slowly, "So it shouldn't be taking this long. It has cooled off in here, so I know she took care of the furnace. She must have gone back to the room to change clothes. I'm going to go upstairs and check. You guys wait here. I'll be right back." And she ran off down the hall.

In the basement, Jane worked at freeing her foot. At first she was merely annoyed. Soaking wet and chilled to the bone, all she wanted was to get back to her room and into dry clothes. She couldn't believe the only thing preventing her from doing just that was a stupid garden hose hidden under a couple of inches of water. But as she bent to pull the hose away from her ankle and found its coils cold and unyielding, her annoyance began to escalate to panic. It should have taken only seconds to slip the foot free of its snare. Instead, stiff, cold fingers met stiff, cold hose and the result was no progress at all. Her hands were too numb with cold to do much good and the hose wasn't giving an inch. The ankle remained imprisoned.

"This is ridiculous!" Jane cried, standing up straight to ease her aching back. Shivering, she stared down at her ice-cold feet, ankle-deep in the dark water. "My toes are probably turning blue!" Could frostbite occur from standing too long in cold water instead of ice or snow? She had no idea. But shooting pains in her trapped right leg made the prospect seem likely.

If only she hadn't turned off the furnace. At least she'd be *warm*. A sodden pajama and robe were no protection at all from the damp chill of the basement. She shivered again.

"This is so stupid!" she told the uncaring furnace. Its ugly black form stared at her silently. "No one is going to believe I was held captive by a stupid garden hose!"

Behind her, there was a throbbing sound, like a steady, quiet murmuring of a distant drum. She turned her head. The log "plug" she had inserted in the stone wall was being hammered at mercilessly by the storm's over-flow. The log was being pushed steadily out of its snug harbor, and the water flowing in from outside continued to push at it.

"No!" Jane cried sharply as the log inched forward. "You get right back in there! The last thing in the world I need now is a flood in this dumb basement!"

But her words were drowned out by a loud pop! as the plug gave way to a sudden gush of water, leaped out of its hole and landed at Jane's feet.

"Oh, no!" she moaned. Storm water began pouring into the basement in a steady stream. It suddenly occurred to Jane that if the water continued to rush in at such an astonishing volume and she remained trapped where she was . . . couldn't she drown? Merrie had said the basement had previously been flooded to the stairs. Glancing up nervously, Jane real-ized that the stairs were certainly higher than sixty-five inches. Jane Barrett was sixty-five inches tall.

Panic set in and she kicked wildly, desper-ately trying to free her foot. She was amazed at how painful her actions were. The ankle must have swelled. Bending down once more,

Jane stuck both hands into the chilly water and fumbled with her captor. The more she pulled and tugged under the water, the tighter the rubber noose around her ankle seemed to get. The water inching up her legs at an alarming rate made her actions unusually clumsy. Tears of frustration sprang to her eyes. She wasn't getting anywhere.

I'll have to drag the whole stupid hose with me, she decided. I can't just stand here while this basement floods. Aware that even if she could drag the whole tangled mess over to the stone steps, she'd probably never get it up them, she decided to try, anyway. She had to do something!

But when she moved her left foot to begin her trek over to the stone steps, that, too, became entangled in the treacherous coils of the hose.

"I don't believe this," she said, her voice quietly frantic. The log that had plugged the hole in the wall swirled by her, banging painfully at her shin as it passed.

"Ouch!" Tears of pain filled her eyes. "I can't take any more of this!" There was only one thing left to do. Sodden and chilled from her toes to her head and beginning to feel a very real fear rising in her along with the level of the water in the basement, Jane opened her mouth.

"Help!" she shouted at the top of her lungs, "Somebody, please! I need help!"

CHAPTER TWENTY-ONE

Upstairs, one floor above Jane, Andy called to Toby and the two boys, "Shh! Listen! Did you hear something?" They were directly opposite the door to the basement.

Cary shook his head no. "All I hear," he said, "is the rain hammering down against the windows and a bunch of girls at the other end of the hall."

"No, there it is again!" Andy insisted. Her eyes were very wide. "It's someone calling for help."

"That's our Andy," Matt teased, putting an arm around her shoulders. "Always finding melodrama in every situation. You should be an actress instead of a dancer." But Andy didn't smile. She was so insistent that they all stood still and listened.

The voice sounded very far away. "Help! Somebody, I need help!"

"That's Jane," Andy said quickly. "She's in the basement. C'mon!"

They rushed to the door. Cary yanked on the knob. Nothing happened. He tried again. "It's stuck! Matt, you pull on me when I pull on the door." Matt obeyed, but in vain. The door remained firmly shut.

"Somebody, please! Get me out of here!"

"Jane," Toby shouted through the door, "we're coming! We'll be right there."

"But how? How are we going to get to Jane if we can't even get the door open?" Toby asked.

"We could take off the hinges," Matt offered.

"Except for a few hammers, the tools are all down in the basement," Toby reminded him. "We can't take a door off the hinges without tools."

The four of them stood together in silent gloom. Jane had stopped calling. They all knew it was because she expected her rescuers to appear at any moment.

"Wait a sec," Toby cried, "there's another door!"

Matt frowned. "To the basement? Where?"

"It's an outside entrance. It's just a little door, but we've used it before. Merrie said they used to bring coal in that way, a long time ago. We can use it to get to Jane."

"Well, get your raincoats, then," Andy ordered. "It's pouring out there!"

Cary moved close to the basement door and called, "Jane, relax! We'll be there in a few minutes. Just stay right where you are."

In the basement, Jane tilted her head toward the sound of Cary's voice. As cold and exhausted and scared as she was, she found herself laughing aloud as Cary's words registered. "Stay where I *am*?" she said to the furnace. "Is he kidding? Does he really think I'd still be in this crummy underground dungeon if I had a choice?" Just knowing help was on its way made laughter possible. What on earth was Cary doing here, anyway? Had he come to Canby through this awful storm? Must be someone here he'd been worried about. Just thinking that made Jane feel a little bit warmer.

Her four rescuers gasped as the full brunt of the storm slammed into them on Baker House's front stoop. "You came all the way over here in *this*?" Andy shouted, hugging her yellow slicker close around her. "You're lucky you weren't blown away or drowned. This is the worst storm I've ever seen."

"Me, too," Toby agreed. "It's a real gully-washer."

The other three glanced at her with curiosity, but there wasn't time for her to explain the term. "Let's all hold hands," she yelled, "so we don't get separated." The wind howling around them, slapping sheets of rain against them, fortified her suggestion. They joined hands. Lowering their heads against the wind, they began inching their way around to the side of Baker House. Thoroughly wet within seconds, they stayed close to the building, trying to avoid the worst of the storm.

When they reached the little arched doorway, they had one brief bad moment when they came face-to-face with a shiny gold padlock hanging on the wrought iron latch. "Oh, no!" Andy cried.

"It's okay," Cary said hastily. "Look, it's not fastened. Whoever put the tools back last probably forgot to fasten the padlock."

Grateful for those girls at Canby Hall who didn't always do as they'd been told, Andy pulled the little door open. No one had remembered to bring a flashlight, and there were no windows in the little passageway to the main basement. It was pitch-black in the narrow corridor. But they kept going. By the time they reached the stone steps leading down to the main room of the basement, water was swirling around Jane's kneecaps.

"Jane," Toby called from the top step as Jane's face lit up with relief, "why on earth are you standing there in all that water? I know the door at the top of the stairs is stuck, but you could have come up here where it's dry."

Jane uttered a strange sound. "I'm prospecting for gold, Toby," she cried. "If you join me, I'll split my findings with you fifty-fifty."

The four rescuers stood silently at the top of the stone steps, staring down at the sorry sight of a sodden, shivering Jane.

"Oh, honestly!" she cried impatiently, "haven't you figured out yet that I'm *stuck* here? Would any sane person be standing in all this muck if they didn't have to? Get me *out* of here!"

Unmindful of certain damage to shoes or jeans, her friends hurried down the steps and waded through the mini-lake to their friend.

"What are you stuck in?" Cary asked innocently, peering down into the dark water. "They keep animal traps down here?"

"Of course not," Jane answered, shaking wet hair back from her face. "No one at Canby goes hunting. I'm stuck in a . . . in a garden hose. And the first person who laughs is going to be really sorry."

"A hose?" Andy wasn't laughing. She was remembering the day she'd filled the dunk tank. She was remembering, with a heavy feeling in her chest, that she and Matt had carelessly tossed the hose down the stairs instead of replacing it on the wall rack. "You're stuck in a garden hose?"

Jane nodded. "I never even saw it. It was buried underneath the water. I must have stepped into a little loop in the hose, and when I tried to pull my foot out, the loop tightened. Then my ankle started swelling and there was no way I could get out after that. My fingers were just too cold and stiff to do much good. And now the other foot is stuck in one of the coils, too."

Andy avoided Matt's eyes. She was hoping

he wouldn't remember. But then, it hadn't been *his* responsibility to replace the hose, so he probably wasn't even thinking about it.

"Listen, Cary," Jane added earnestly as she leaned on Andy for support, "we'd better do something about all this water pouring into the basement. I stuck a log into that hole in the wall, but it popped back out."

"Don't worry about it. First we'll get you unstuck, then we'll worry about Niagara Falls over there. Now," Cary said as he crouched in the water, "where are your feet?"

Jane managed a weak giggle. "At the end of my legs," she said giddily. She hadn't realized how exhausted she was until she'd leaned on Andy. It felt so good to have someone propping her up. Then it struck her that she really needed to lie down. In fact, she needed to lie down more than she needed to eat or to make up with Cary. She was very, very tired.

But it became crystal-clear within minutes that she wouldn't be lying down just yet. Because Cary and Toby and Matt were having a difficult time working the hose coils away from Jane's ankles. The first time anyone's fingers came into contact with flesh rubbed raw by her efforts to escape, Jane screamed. The sound shocked all of them, echoing through the cavern-like basement and bouncing off the walls. Cary's face went chalk-white. He jumped up and hugged Jane to him. "I'm sorry, I'm sorry," he murmured.

"Don't stop trying," she whispered when

she could get her breath. She tried a laugh, but it stuck in her throat. "I'd rather be in pain from swollen ankles than from drowning." It struck all of them then that it wasn't such a far-fetched possibility. The rain hadn't let up in intensity. They could still hear it battering the building. Nor had the gush of water entering through the hole in the wall lessened. If Cary had gone down on his knees to work on the hose, the water would have reached his neck. Instead, he half-bent, half-crouched, reaching beneath the water to pull on the coils trapping Jane's ankles.

"Matt," Cary said, looking up, "we'd better not wait to plug up that hole. Toby and I can untangle this hose. You look around and see what you can find to stop that waterfall."

Matt nodded. "Right. I'll try Jane's log idea again. Sounds like it might work. Maybe I can wedge it in somehow."

While Matt waded through the water in search of the log, Cary bent to try once more to free Jane. As he tugged as gently as he could on the cold, stiff coils, Jane's face turned the color of smoke. She bit through the skin on her bottom lip, drawing blood. But she didn't make a sound.

Andy, supporting Jane and feeling her rigid efforts to keep from screaming, felt horrible. This was all *her* fault. If she hadn't been so careless and irresponsible, Jane wouldn't be in this miserable situation.

"I'm sorry, Jane," she said quietly. But it

was at that instant that Toby and Cary, with one final tug, set Jane's left leg free, and her scream pierced the air, drowning out Andy's apology. Gasping for breath, Jane sagged against Andy, gripping her upper arms so tightly that Andy's fingers went numb.

"The other leg won't be as bad," Toby said gently, lifting her head to look up at Jane with sympathy in her eyes. "Setting your left leg free loosened all of the coils. We'll try not to hurt you this time."

"There!" Matt cried, startling all of them. He patted the end of the log now plugging up the hole. "Now I'm just going to wedge a board across it to hold it in place. That should do the trick." He had already found the right-sized board as Cary and Toby finished freeing Jane.

"You were right," Jane breathed when the second leg had been freed. "That one wasn't so bad." But her oval face was still the color of biscuits. She relinquished her hold on Andy to lean on Cary and added softly, "Will someone please take me upstairs now? I'm very cold."

Toby frowned. "I wish we didn't have to take her outside. She's already soaked. She'll catch pneumonia out there."

"We don't," Andy said firmly, "and we're not going to." She waded over to the wall, grabbed an axe and took the stairs two at a time. When she reached the stubborn door leading into the hall, she gave the panel closest to the knob two solid whacks. The sound of splintering wood echoed throughout the basement. One more blow, and the door flew open. Light streamed into the basement from the first floor. A cheer rose up from the group waiting below.

"Okay, let's go!" Andy called. Cary scooped Jane up in his arms, saying, "You're in no shape to climb those stairs." He meant because she had to be very tired, but when he saw her ankles protruding from the rolled-up pajamas draped over his arm, he realized that even a limitless supply of energy wouldn't have propelled Jane up the stairs. Not on those ankles. Andy and Toby gasped and Matt said softly, "Oh, wow."

Both ankles were swollen to twice their normal size. They had already begun to discolor and the hose had scraped off more than one layer of skin during Jane's struggles to escape.

My fault, Andy thought, tears in her eyes, my fault.

"C'mon, let's get this girl upstairs," Cary said, his face grim. He led the way, Toby and Andy right behind him. Matt gave the log a final pat, and followed.

Upstairs in Room 407, Cary deposited Jane gently on her bed while Toby ran to get Meredith. Then Cary left so Andy could help Jane dry off and slip into warm, dry clothing.

"Oh, Jane," was all Merrie said when she saw the results of Jane's stay in the basement.

Then she hurried off to get first-aid equipment.

"This," Jane told her with a tiny grin when she came back to tend to the bruised and raw ankles, "is the kind of story people laugh about . . . later. After it's all over. I mean, can you imagine *me* telling my grandchildren I was held hostage in the basement by a garden hose?"

Andy and Toby, sitting quietly on their beds, didn't laugh.

"Come on, you guys," Jane urged, wincing as Merrie applied antiseptic to her wounds, "you've gotta admit it's funny. Kind of Twilight-Zonish, right?"

Andy burst into tears.

There was an awkward silence. Then Jane said, "Correct me if I'm wrong, but isn't the wrong person crying here? Andy, what's the matter?"

Andy wiped her face with a corner of her bedspread. "It's all my fault," she said, trying and failing to keep her eyes away from Jane's poor ankles. "I left that hose there. I meant to go back down and put it on the rack later, but I forgot. And . . . and saying I'm sorry just doesn't do you any good at all, does it?"

"No," Jane said calmly, as Merrie rolled white gauze around her left ankle. "I think you'll just have to be shot."

Toby laughed, but Andy wailed. "I know I should. I really should. You had such an awful time down there and your poor ankles look like chopped liver, and I wouldn't blame you if you never forgave me!"

"Yes, you would," Jane replied. "I know you, Andrea Cord, you always expect people to forgive you because *you* always forgive *them*. Even me. And I've done some pretty stupid things, or have you forgotten? Or," with a grin, "do you only forget things like putting hoses where they belong?"

"Ouch!" Andy said, a sheepish grin overtaking her tears.

Jane shrugged. "You had that one coming." Merrie had finished her repair work and Jane relaxed against the pillow, luxuriating in the feeling of being warm and dry. "Look, Andy, it's over and done with. And you don't have to worry about it ever happening again, because I don't intend to ever go near that basement again."

As Jane closed her eyes, Merrie signaled to Toby and Andy to leave the room with her. Outside in the hall, she whispered, "She needs to rest. Come and help me see how much food the girls have gathered together. We're not going to get to the Dining Hall for a while."

Outside, the rain continued to pound Baker House.

Jane slept.

CHAPTER TWENTY-TWO

Matt and Cary spent the rest of the day with the Canby Hall students waiting for the rain to end. Some students gathered in the first-floor parlor, entertaining themselves with games of Clue, Trivial Pursuit, or checkers. Staving off hunger by nibbling on the collection of goodies gathered from care packages earlier in the day, they waited out the storm. When Jane awoke, Cary went upstairs to sit with her and keep her company.

It was late afternoon when the rain tapered off and, finally, ended. Only a steady drip-drip from the roof remained. The last of the clouds scattered, revealing a pale, watery sun overhead.

"Well," Matt said as they all stood silently looking out the window, "we might as well go check out the damage. Better wear hipboots, though. The whole campus could be one big lake after all that rain."

No one had hip boots. But they were all

anxious to see what the storm had done to their campus and to their carnival preparations. With the exception of Jane and Cary, the residents of Baker House followed Matt outside.

It was worse than any of them had imagined. There seemed to be water everywhere. Broken tree limbs and branches floated in puddles of muddy brown, and even where there were no small lakes, the ground was so saturated their feet made loud squishing sounds as they walked.

Toby glanced around her. "Will it ever dry out?"

"Oh, sure," Matt said. "It'll take a day or two, though. It'll be a muddy mess until then. Let's go see what's left of our carnival handiwork."

They reached the dunk tank first. Although it was still in place, as Andy had known it would be, it sat, smug and fat, in a murky pool of its own overflow. "Ugh!" Andy declared, checking the Tank's contents by peering over its edge. "I wouldn't make my worst enemy climb into this icky stuff. It'll have to be emptied out and refilled." That reminded her of the evil garden hose, and she shuddered. Well, at least Jane had forgiven her. Now all she had to do was forgive herself. Jane's ankles were such a mess!

Upstairs in Room 407, Jane was thinking exactly the same thing. She was resting in bed, propped up by a bed pillow, and was feeling warm and safe. Although the antique quilt covered her legs, the bandaged ankles were uncovered. "They feel like they got caught in a cement mixer," she told Cary. He was sitting on a chair beside her bed. Although the door was wide open according to Baker House rules, everyone had gone outside, so the hall was quiet.

"They hurt, huh?" he asked, his blue eyes sympathetic.

She shrugged. "I'll survive." She thought for a minute before adding, "I feel sorry for Andy, though. I mean, she feels really bad about leaving that stupid hose lying at the foot of the stairs."

Cary smiled and reached for her hand. "I thought I heard you say something about 'stupid carelessness' when we first reached you in the basement."

Jane grinned. "I suppose I did. I was feeling pretty miserable and I *was* mad. But when I saw how awful she felt, how could I stay mad? I know she never meant to cause any trouble. Not Andy. She just wasn't thinking that day they had the hose, that's all."

Cary squeezed her hand. "You know," he said, "you still surprise me sometimes. I think that's what I like most about you. Just when I think you're predictable, you're not. You're full of surprises."

"Good! 'Consistency is the hobgoblin of

little minds,'" she quoted mischievously.
"How boring!"

"Jane, you may be lots of things, but you're
not boring."

She didn't ask him what the "lots of things"
were. She wasn't sure she wanted to know.
Instead, she said, "Well, I wonder what's
happened to our carnival work?"

"I don't believe this," Andy moaned, surveying the remains of their hard work. Of the
ten completed booths, only one remained
intact."

"It's not so bad," Matt said quietly. He
put a comforting arm around her shoulders.
"If we can find the pieces, and they aren't
splintered, we can just nail them back together again."

Andy shook away his arm and took a step
backward. "Oh, you're always so calm!" she
said angrily, out of fatigue and guilt and disappointment. "That just drives me crazy!"
Her dark eyes shone with unshed tears. "All
of our hard work has been blitzed right out
of existence. Why don't you scream and holler
because it's all so unfair?"

Unperturbed, Matt answered calmly, "Because it wouldn't do any good. But if it makes
you feel better, go ahead."

Andy knew Matt was just being his usual
logical self. Wasn't that one of the things she'd
always liked about him? His calmness? So why

was she picking on him now? Because she needed desperately to lash out at someone or something, to explode, to let her anger and frustration loose. If it stayed inside, it would choke her. But it really wasn't fair to vent it on Matt. None of this was his fault.

"I'm sorry," she apologized. "You're right." But as she stared at the spot where their booths had stood, she made a decision. "But I can't just accept everything that's happened. If we're going to have any carnival at all, we're going to need help." She took a deep breath and let it out. "I'm going to go see P.A."

"What for? How will that help?"

Andy shook her head. "I don't know. But she's probably just as upset about this mess as we are. Maybe she can figure out where we can get some help." Her voice gathered strength. "And if she can't, then she'll just have to call off the strike, that's all. We need those maintenance people and we need them now!"

"Atta girl, Andy!" Dee called from the group surrounding Andy and Matt. "You tell 'er!"

Andy's face grew hot. She hadn't realized everyone in the group was listening.

"Well, I'm going with you," Toby said, leaving no room for argument.

Andy accepted the offer gratefully. Turning to Matt, she said, "How about if the rest

of you start looking for pieces of our missing
booths? While Toby and I tackle P.A., you
can collect whatever's left of our lumber.
We'll help you when we get back."

"Sure." He put a hand on her elbow. "Good
luck," he said quietly, and kissed her cheek.

"Thanks. C'mon, Toby. Might as well get
right to it."

Walking through debris and puddles toward the Administration Building, Toby
asked Andy what she was going to say to
their headmistress. "You can't just walk into
her office and tell her to call off the strike,
can you?"

Andy shrugged. "Well, I won't say it like
that. I *can* be tactful, Toby. I *do* know how."

Toby's only comment was a silent grin.

"I'll just tell her we can't keep going without some help." Andy stepped over a fallen
tree limb. "We've done our best. And I, for
one, think we've done pretty well. But this
storm was just one problem too many."

Toby frowned. "Do you really think we
can't have the carnival if the strike isn't called
off?"

"I don't see how we can. In fact," Andy
added grimly, "with this mess on campus and
all of those broken windows, P.A. has probably already decided to close Canby Hall."

"Oh, no, she couldn't. Not after all our
hard work, trying to keep it open."

Oh, but she could, they discovered after less
than five minutes in her office.

"I'm sorry, girls," a very tired-looking Ms. Allardyce told them, regret heavy in her voice. She stood at the window looking out across campus, a tall, strong figure in tan trousers and sweater. "I just took my own tour of the campus. I feel I have no choice. I can't have my girls staying in dormitory rooms without windows."

"Then end the strike!" Andy cried, desperation erasing all caution. "Just *end* it, so the maintenance people can come back to work. They'll fix the windows."

"I can't do that."

Andy flashed a look of anger at Toby. How could P.A. be so stubborn? Well, Andrea Cord could be stubborn, too. No matter what the consequences might be, she wasn't leaving this office without saying what she felt. P.A. had told them more than once that there was no such word as "can't."

Hoping her headmistress had meant that, Andy said clearly, "I don't see why you can't. Unless you really want Canby Hall to close."

Toby gasped. A sudden flash of pain crossed Ms. Allardyce's handsome, strong-boned face, surprising Andy. Turning, the woman faced the two girls. I just hurt her, Andy thought with certainty, but I'm not sure how or why.

"You thought *I* could end this strike?" the headmistress asked, dismay in her blue eyes. "Have you thought that all along? Is that what all of the girls think?"

Andy, for once, was speechless. She was beginning to wish she'd never come near this office. All she seemed to be doing today was hurting people.

"Andrea," Ms. Allardyce said softly, "I have nothing to do with this labor dispute. I thought you girls understood that. It's strictly between the employees and the Board of Trustees." She was silent for a moment, hands clasped in front of her. Then she added, almost in a murmur, "What you must all think of me! But," and they saw disappointment in her eyes, "how could any of you believe I would let this situation continue if I had any power to stop it?"

Toby flushed and worked at memorizing the pattern in the carpet at her feet. Andy cringed inwardly at the look of hurt on her headmistress's face, knowing she was responsible for it. She wasn't sure she could undo the damage she had done, but she had to try.

"I'm really sorry, Ms. Allardyce," she said, taking a step forward. "We just didn't understand. I guess we should have asked who was really responsible."

"No." Ms. Allardyce shook her head. "Thank you for saying so, but it was my job to explain. I see that now. I should have talked more about it to all of you. I'm afraid I was so preoccupied with our problems I wasn't concerned enough with what you might be thinking about my role in this."

"Well," Toby said loyally, "it's a big job

running Canby even when there isn't a strike. You probably didn't have time to talk to us."

"That's no excuse." She walked over to her desk and stood behind it. "All I can say is, I'm very sorry." She looked directly at Andy. "Do you understand now?"

Andy hesitated. Honesty was still probably the best policy. She thought of her friends and fellow students outside hunting through muddy puddles for pieces of lumber. "No," she said clearly, "I really don't understand. I mean," she added hastily, "I understand about none of this being your fault. I apologize for thinking such a thing in the first place. I know you care about Canby Hall."

"Thank you, Andrea."

"But I still don't understand why the strike goes on and on. I know the workers don't want that. Why hasn't someone *done* something? Why doesn't the Board of Trustees just end it? They can do that, can't they?"

The headmistress nodded. "Yes, of course they can. But they're . . . well, they just don't seem inclined to do so. They don't want to give in to the strikers' demands."

Andy made a sound of disgust. "Well, that's just plain stupid! All the employees want is to get their old hours back. And they should have them. It's the only way they can get all their work done."

There was silence for a few moments. Then Andy said abruptly, "What are their names?"

"I beg your pardon?"

"The names of the Board members. Could you give them to me? And their addresses, please?"

Ms. Allardyce raised well-groomed eyebrows. "May I ask why you want them?"

"Sure. I'm going to do some person-to-person negotiating of my own. This school can't take another day of this stupid strike."

"You plan to go see the Board members?"

"Yes, I do," Andy answered firmly. Then, not so firmly, "You're not going to tell me I can't, are you? I mean, I wouldn't be breaking any rules, would I?"

Ms. Allardyce hesitated. Then the barest hint of a smile played around her lips. "No, I have never heard of such a rule. Perhaps there's never been a need for one."

And if by that she meant she'd never had such a crazy student before, then that was all right with Andy. As long as she got what she wanted.

She did. And as she left the headmistress's office with a piece of paper clutched tightly in her hand, six names and addresses printed clearly on it, Ms. Allardyce called after her, "I wish you luck!"

And then, although Andy didn't hear her, she added as she closed the door, "But I don't think you're the ones who are going to need it."

And she let the smile tugging at her lips escape.

CHAPTER
TWENTY-THREE

A ndy and Toby decided it was too late, not to mention too wet, that day to head for town. They would get a good night's sleep and tackle the Board of Trustees the next day. They said nothing to an exhausted Jane about their plans. She had enough to think about. Instead, they made sure she was covered well, then went to bed themselves. It had been a very long day.

The next morning, they left for the Dining Hall before Jane had awakened and when they returned, they burst into Room 407 and rushed straight to the closet. Cary had already arrived to visit with Jane. They stared as Jane's roommates rifled through the closet.

"What does one wear to a begging session," Toby asked Andy, grinning.

"We're *not* going to beg," Andy replied, fingering a blue silk blouse. "Well, maybe just a little. We'd better wear something that protects our legs, now that you mention it, just in case we have to kneel."

"What on earth is going on?" Jane cried. "What are you two up to?"

Andy turned to face her, a pink sweater in her hands. "I guess you could say we're going to a Board meeting."

Jane frowned.

Andy grinned at Toby. "Well, we're going to meet with all six members of the Board of Trustees, so I guess that's a Board meeting, right?"

"You guys are going to tackle the Board members?" Cary asked.

Andy nodded. "Yes, and you have to leave so Toby and I can change our clothes. Go hang out in the hall. We'll call you when we're decent."

He stood up. "You're really serious about this, aren't you?"

"Yes, we are. We're sick to death of this strike business. And when you see what that storm did to this campus, you'll know why we just can't keep going without help. P.A. had already decided to close Canby when we got to her office."

Jane's eyes widened. "She knows you're going into town? To see the Board members?"

This time, it was Toby who nodded. "And *I* think she's all for it. She's just as sick of the strike as we are, but she can't do anything about it. I think she's glad we're going."

"Well, *I'm* coming, too!" Jane threw her

comforter aside and attempted to swing her legs to the floor. But she couldn't smother a moan as she did so and pain lines were clearly visible around her mouth.

"No, Jane," Andy said firmly, pulling the comforter back in place. "You've done your part this weekend. You can't walk on those ankles, anyway."

"Besides," Toby added gently, "you've earned a rest after the miserable time you had in the basement. You just wish us luck and keep your fingers crossed, okay? We'll tell you all about it when we get back."

Jane wasn't happy with that, but she knew her roommates were right. She wouldn't be of much use to them when she couldn't even walk without hobbling.

"I'll stay here with you, Jane," Cary promised. "We have a lot to talk about, anyway."

"Well, that's fine," Andy said, "but first Toby and I have to change. You can go call Matt for us and ask him to come over here and drive us into town. If we walk, we'll be all muddy by the time we face our enemy, and that would be a definite disadvantage."

Cary left, promising Jane he'd be right back.

The girls chose flannel trousers, sweaters, and blazers with the Canby Hall emblem on the pocket. Each of them gave Jane a comforting hug before they left the room. They knew how hard it was for her to remain behind.

Although they often teased her about being a spoiled rich kid, she wasn't the kind of person who let other people do her dirty work. This time, she had no choice.

They passed Cary in the hall. He wished them luck, telling them Matt was on his way.

While they waited outside for him, they glanced around campus. Much of the lumber from the broken booths had been found. It sat in a damp pile beside the dunk tank. Volunteers in old clothes were sloshing through puddles collecting debris from the storm, filling black plastic bags with litter.

Andy sighed. "At least the sun is out," she told Toby. "That should help dry things up." But privately she was wondering if the Canby Hall campus she loved would ever be the same.

Matt pulled up in front of them. The girls looked at each other, took deep breaths, and got into the car.

The first address on Andy's list belonged to a man named Barstow. Matt said he knew him. Maneuvering the car skillfully around the deepest mud puddles, he said, "He owns the electrical supply store in town. I've been in there a lot."

Andy asked the obvious question. "What's he like?"

Matt shrugged. "He's okay, I guess. Not exactly Mr. Warmth, but he's no Genghis Khan, either. Just be honest with him." He grinned. "That is, *if* he lets you in the front door."

When they reached the house, Matt wanted to come in with them, but Andy said no. "This is our job," she insisted. "But if you really don't mind driving us around this afternoon, we'd really appreciate it. If you don't have other stuff to do."

Matt had plenty of other stuff to do, but he didn't say so. He admired their courage and wanted to help. He would do his other stuff later.

The house was a sturdy, good-looking, two-story brick Tudor. "I smell money," Toby whispered nervously as they approached the front door.

"Well, of course you do. Poor people don't get to serve on Boards." Andy was trembling just a little and her stomach was being struck by lightning every few seconds. What if he yelled at them? What if he tossed them out on their ears? Could he have them arrested? Of course not! They weren't breaking any laws.

But the portly, balding man who answered the door acted as if they were. "I'm eating lunch," he said brusquely, "and I'm not buying anything. Weren't you girls already here selling cookies?"

Andy bit back a nervous giggle. "We're not selling anything, Mr. Barstow. We're from Canby Hall. We'd like to talk to you for a few minutes. It's about the strike."

His round face flushed angrily. "I've got nothing to say about that. Wasn't *my* doing. You blaming me?"

"Oh, no, sir, of course not! If we could just come in and explain. I promise we won't stay long."

An attractive woman with white hair peered over the man's shoulder. She smiled at Andy and Toby. "For heaven's sake, Charles," she said, "stop being such an old grouch and let them in!" As she turned to leave, she poked playfully at his ample stomach. "You don't need that second piece of pie, anyway."

Grumbling in the direction of the woman's back as she walked away, Mr. Barstow pulled the door open wider to let Andy and Toby inside. He led them into a huge living room off the hall. It was wallpapered in a tiny floral print and filled with antiques.

"Excuse us for interrupting your Sunday at home, sir," Andy began, wishing he would ask them to sit down. He didn't. He stood in front of a wood-paneled fireplace, hands behind his back, his eyes expressionless behind glasses. "But we feel that you might not be aware of the situation at Canby Hall. We're students there and we love it and we don't want to see it closed because of the strike."

"Hmph!" He adjusted the bow-tie he was wearing with his white shirt. "Should have been closed the minute those workers walked off the job, if you ask me."

"Oh, no, sir," Toby said firmly, "it shouldn't have." Andy nodded her support. "I came all the way from Texas," Toby continued, "to get my education at Canby and it's a good education. A whole lot of hurt would be done by closing the school."

When she mentioned Texas, the man's expression indicated clearly that he thought Texas should be closed down along with Canby Hall. But he must have been listening, because when she'd finished, he said, "Oh? Then suppose you girls tell me what you think should be done."

The two roommates exchanged glances. Go for it, Andy's dark eyes seemed to say. So Toby did. "The workers should be given back their normal hours. We've personally learned just how much work they have to do. The shorter schedule your Board has given them just won't let them get done all the stuff they're supposed to do."

Mr. Barstow remained silent. Encouraged because they hadn't been thrown out, Toby continued, "And now that everything's such a mess because of that terrible storm, we need the workers back more than ever." Shrugging helplessly, she added, "We just can't keep going without their help."

Andy had been listening attentively to Toby's plea. Now, she added her own. "And while you're calling off the strike," she added boldly, "you might even think about giving them a little raise."

The man's lips clamped together, but Andy hurried on. "The price of everything has gone up, sir, as I'm sure you know." She was tempted to glance pointedly at some of the antiques, but decided against it. Why offend him more than she already had? "Most of the workers are raising families. If you would just think about it? You look like a fair-minded man. Just a little bit more money and their old hours back would send the employees right back to work, I'm sure of it."

"She's right," Toby agreed. "Then Canby Hall could stay open, and we could still have our Almost Summer Carnival."

The man surprised them then by letting a dreamy expression float across his face. "Ah, yes, the carnival," he murmured absent-mindedly. "Been having that at Canby since I was a boy. Had some good times there."

Andy eye-signaled to Toby, Can you imagine *him* as a boy? But they were both careful not to smile.

"Sit down, sit down," he said then, waving them toward an upholstered couch opposite the fireplace. "Won't hurt to discuss this a bit more, since you've already interrupted my Sunday."

And he listened to every word as Andy and Toby earnestly explained why they felt the strikers were entitled to their old hours and more pay. Andy mentioned things like old plumbing and electricity, requiring a great deal of maintenance, and the responsibility of keeping so many girls well-fed and well-cared for. When she ran out of breath, Toby assisted her, fortifying Andy's arguments. Occasionally, the man nodded or har-umphed, but he made no comments.

When the girls finally remembered poor Matt, sitting outside in the car probably thinking they'd both been murdered and tossed out the back door, they stood up. "We have to go now," Andy said. "We still have the other Board members to see. Thank you for listening. I hope you'll think about everything we've said."

He made them no promises. But as he saw them to the door, he asked, "Going to barge in on all five of them, are you?"

Andy nodded.

"Well, good luck with Tucker. You'll need it. He's a tough old bird."

Andy swallowed hard, thanked him again for his time, and followed Toby out to the car.

They needn't have worried about the "tough old bird," Tucker, because he refused to let them into his house. "Barstow phoned me," he said in a thin, chilly voice. "Said I should see you, hear what you have to say. Well, forget it. I'm busy. Go away. Go back to that school of yours and do some studying."

"Mr. Tucker," Toby said boldly, "it won't do us any good to study if we don't have a school to attend." But he'd already closed the door.

They refused to let that discourage them. Mr. Barstow had told Tucker he should see them, so mightn't that mean Barstow was on their side? At least a little? They couldn't give up now.

As if to make up for Mr. Tucker's rudeness, they got lucky at the next address. Three of the remaining four Board members were having lunch there. And although none gave any indication of their reaction to the girls' pleas, they did promise to pass the message on to Lucy Danby, the final Board member. Two trustees had asked some intelligent questions, and one, Ms. McGill, had actually smiled.

But none had said they would call off the strike.

"Well," Andy told Matt and Toby when they were in the car heading for Canby Hall, "we *did* try. Now all we can do is wait, and hope like crazy that they really were listening."

Lost in thought, no one talked much during the ride home.

Sometime during that ride home, the telephone rang in Baker House in one of the fourth-floor rooms. The girl who ran to answer it said, "Who? Jane Barrett? No, her telephone line is out, from the storm, I guess. I don't know how you got this room. No. I'm afraid she can't possibly come to the telephone. She had an accident yesterday and it's hard for her to walk. Can I take a message?"

Then she stood back from the telephone, surprise on her face, because the other party had abruptly hung up.

Less than five minutes later, Meredith Pembroke knocked softly on the open door of Room 407 and, in answer to Jane's "Come in," entered the room. Her eyes were sympathetic as she stood beside Jane's bed and said, "Jane. I'm sorry. I've just spoken to your mother. Your parents are coming for you Wednesday night when your father returns from a business trip."

Jane sat up in bed, her eyes wide. "But why? Why now?" A twinge from one of the injured ankles reminded her. She sank back on her pillow. "Oh, no. Who *told* her?"

Meredith sighed. "Carla. It really wasn't her fault, Jane. She didn't realize you hadn't told your parents. Your mother called me immediately after hanging up on poor Carla."

Jane sniffed. "Poor Carla? *She's* not being yanked out of here and taken home like a two-year-old."

"I tried to tell your mother you were fine, but I had a feeling she wasn't really listening to me. I'm sorry, Jane." And knowing there wasn't anything else to say, she left Jane and Cary alone.

Cary put his arms around her, and let her cry on his shoulder.

CHAPTER TWENTY-FOUR

When Andy and Toby arrived back on campus, a great deal had been done to clean up the havoc wreaked by the storm. Fallen tree limbs and branches had disappeared, along with other debris from the wind and rain. The sun, now beginning its descent in the sky, had done its part by drying up the smaller puddles. But the ground was still spongy, and the pile of lumber sat untouched on the lawn, telling them that Cary had decided it was too wet to begin the booth reconstruction.

"Maybe this whole day has been a total waste of time," Andy said gloomily as they climbed Baker House's steps. "Maybe we spent most of the day on a wild goose chase."

"Maybe, but at least we did our best," Toby said. She was tired and the strain showed around her eyes and mouth. "And you were awfully convincing. The Board could still change its mind and end the strike."

Andy glanced at her. "In time for the carnival? We need help *now*! In case you've forgotten, our Almost Summer Carnival is supposed to begin on Wednesday. This is Sunday, Toby."

"I know." They climbed the stairs to 407 in gloomy silence. "Well," Toby added as they opened the door to their room, "at least things can't get much worse. They almost *have* to get better from now on."

But when they walked into their room, they found Jane sitting on her bed staring at her bandaged ankles with morbid fascination. They could see she'd been crying. Her eyes were red and swollen.

"What's wrong?" Andy asked, concern in her voice. She still felt guilty about Jane's accident. "Are you in a lot of pain?"

Jane lifted her head. "Yeah, but it's not my ankles. My parents are coming to get me Wednesday night."

Andy sank down on her own bed. "What?"

Jane explained. "Cary helped me out to the phone and I called her. I told her I was doing just fine. But she wasn't listening. I can always tell when she's not listening because she's talking while *I'm* talking. I might just as well have been talking to one of your stuffed animals, Andy."

The trio sat in gloomy silence.

"Maybe it's just as well," Jane said in a dull voice. "It doesn't look like we're going to have our carnival, after all. And even if we did, I don't know how much help I'd be with two ankles that look like bruised tennis balls."

That reminded Andy that while they were all depressed, Jane had more reason than any of them to be miserable. "Did it hurt really bad to walk to the telephone?"

Jane shrugged. Tired of pajamas, she had exchanged them earlier for pale blue trousers and matching Fair Isle sweater. "Not as much as talking to my mother did."

"Think you can make it to the Dining Hall? Or would you rather we just brought you something to eat?"

"No, I'll come. I need to get out of this room. That dumb gray blanket on the window is so depressing. It shuts out all the light. I'll just walk really slow, okay? You guys will have to be patient with me."

The atmosphere in the Dining Hall was almost as depressing as their room had been. The news that Canby Hall would be closing had spread quickly. Sandwiches lay untouched, soup cooled in bowls.

"I just hate the thought of going to school this summer," Dee complained petulantly. "Summer is for the *beach*. Do you realize that if we have to attend classes this summer, I might not even get a *tan*?"

"Well, I never tan," Maggie said, "but what I'm worried about is, I might not even be able to come back to Canby. Ever! My mother won't like having my education interrupted.

She just might send me somewhere else."

Dee looked horrified. Maggie had been her roommate since September and in spite of their obvious differences, Dee couldn't imagine rooming with anyone else.

"I suppose," Jane said slowly, "that I should at least be grateful for one thing."

Andy lifted her head from the soup she'd been toying with. "What one thing?"

"That dumb pie-baking contest. I won't be here for that." She sighed. "Maybe I would have poisoned a whole bunch of people, so I'm being sent home to save lives. Who knows?"

No one laughed.

"You *would* be here for it if we were having one," Andy argued. "If we were still having the carnival, we'd be baking pies on Tuesday night, and you said your parents aren't coming until Wednesday."

"Well, I might be here," Jane said hotly, "but I certainly wouldn't spend time baking pies for a carnival I wasn't even going to be able to attend!"

They were all sitting in grim silence when the Dining Hall door opened and Ms. Allardyce walked in, followed by Meredith Pembroke and the housemothers from Charles and Addison Houses.

"Oh, no," Andy groaned, "it's official! They've come to make the announcement that Canby is closing. Oh, I can't stand it!" She buried her face in her hands.

Ms. Allardyce, wearing a bright red suit, stood at the front of the hall. "Ladies," she intoned without emotion, "I have an announcement." She hesitated as her students fought tears, and then a smile eased the stern expression on her handsome face. She said clearly, "The strike is over."

The news came as such a shock that no one said anything. No one moved. Eyes wide in disbelief watched as their headmistress repeated, "The strike has been settled. Workers are already returning to campus."

Voices began murmuring then, but the group as a whole still registered disbelief. They had been expecting something entirely different.

"The crews will be repairing windows all evening," Ms. Allardyce continued. "Mr. Lombardi at the lumberyard has graciously consented to stay open long enough to give us the glass we need. Those of you whose windows aren't repaired tonight and have no covering over the open frame will sleep in the halls as you did last night. By tomorrow afternoon, we expect that all of the storm damage will be erased." Her smile broadened. "And I have already spoken with the foreman of the maintenance crew. I've explained to him that his second priority after the window repairs, will be helping you get your carnival back together."

She paused to let her words sink in. And after a minute or two, stunned disbelief was replaced by one enormous sigh of relief. Then screams and shouts of joy shook the Dining Hall to its rafters. There were hugs all around. Andy beamed and Toby slapped her on the back in congratulations. Only Jane's smile seemed less than enthusiastic, which everyone understood since their reprieve had come too late for her.

Ms. Allardyce waited until the commotion had died down before announcing that the entire school owed its deep gratitude to, in particular, the residents of Room 407 in Baker House.

"I would like, at this time, to ask Andrea Cord and October Houston to stand. These girls," she said as the embarrassed roommates obeyed, "tackled the Board of Trustees this afternoon. I don't know exactly what they said, but they must have been very persuasive — which shouldn't surprise those among us who have, at one time or another, been persuaded toward a particular course of action by Andrea Cord."

She means herself, Andy realized, and couldn't resist a grin.

"Shall we give these girls a round of applause?"

There was clapping and shouting, even whistles of appreciation. When it ended and Toby and Andy had resumed their seats, their headmistress said, "One more thing. I realize our carnival is scheduled to begin on Wednesday. Notices have already been printed to that effect. Since it would be difficult if not impossible to inform the public of a change at this late date, I am excusing all Canby Hall students from afternoon classes on Monday, Tuesday, and Wednesday of this week. That should give you the time you need to put things back together."

Another roar of approval filled the dining hall. "Of course," the headmistress said when quiet resumed, "our carnival hours will be as usual: evenings only during the week, from six o'clock until ten o'clock. All day long on the weekend, of course. You will all be expected to attend classes all day on Thursday and Friday."

That news dampened no one's spirits. They could accomplish a lot in three afternoons free of classes. And they wouldn't be doing it completely alone, now that the strike was over. The carpenters were coming back and would be helping.

Andy stood up. "Ms. Allardyce," she said, "we'd all like to thank you. For . . . well, for everything. And we're all really happy that Canby Hall isn't closing."

Everyone nodded. Ms. Allardyce smiled. As she turned to leave, she called, "I expect this carnival to be the best yet. I'm sure after all you've been through because of it, you won't disappoint me."

"No, ma'am," Andy said, "we sure won't."

The headmistress waved a hand and left. All three housemothers went with her.

The door had barely closed behind them when cheering broke out again. Only Jane found it impossible to join in.

"Cheer up!" Andy said as they got up to leave. "Maybe when your folks get here and see that everything is under control, they'll change their minds and let you stay."

Jane scowled as she limped out of the building. "Fat chance!"

"Maybe." Andy thought for a minute as the three girls, arm-in-arm to give Jane needed support, made their way across a twilight-shrouded campus. "I know what!" she exclaimed. "What you need to do is bake a perfectly scrumptious pie! That will surprise them, right?"

"It would certainly surprise *me*," Jane muttered. "Andy, what on earth are you nattering on about?"

Andy began talking very fast. "Look, you bake this terrific pie and that convinces them not only that you're perfectly fine, because you couldn't bake a pie if you were at death's door, could you? And it also tells them that you're learning new things here. They won't make you go home then."

"Sounds sensible to me," Toby said admiringly.

"Except for one thing," Jane argued. "It just so happens I can't *bake* a pie. Not a scrumptious one, not a delicious one, not even a barely edible one."

"Of course you can. Anyone can bake a pie. We'll help."

"Oh, wait a minute, Andy," Toby protested as they reached Baker House. "Speak for yourself. Biscuits are my specialty, not pie."

"Don't be silly! Biscuits are practically the same thing as pie. It's dough, isn't it? You just put things in pie that you don't put in biscuits, right? Anyway," she added airily, "the three of us can do anything we really want to. We got rid of that stupid strike, didn't we?"

"You two did," Jane said, "not me."

Andy held the door open. "If I hadn't felt so guilty about leaving that hose where it could trap you, I might not have gone near a Board member. So you did help, even if you didn't actually go with us."

"Okay, okay," Jane said, giving in. "I'll take a shot at baking a pie. But I can't see something like that changing my mother's mind." When they reached their room, she sat down on her bed. "So when do I get to play Betty Crocker?"

"Tuesday night. We should have most of the other stuff done by then, and we can't work outside after dark, anyway. We'll take over the kitchen in the Dining Hall right after dinner. And the pies will still be fresh on Wednesday for the contest."

Jane looked dubious. But if she was going to be dragged away from Canby Hall on Wednesday, she wanted to spend as much time as possible with her friends. So if they were going to be in the kitchen, so was she, no matter how foolish she might look in a kitchen.

She looked pretty foolish, she had to admit, on Tuesday night. "I look ridiculous!" she wailed as Cary passed her, carrying a colander full of sliced apples. "I'm flour from head to toe!"

"You look cute," he said with a grin, swiping at her flour-covered nose with a dish towel. "But you're supposed to put the flour in the piecrust, Jane, not take a bath in it."

Instead of retorting with a sarcastic remark, Jane grinned. She was having fun and no one was more surprised by that than she was. It was nice, sitting high on a stool beside the butcher-block counter in a nice, warm kitchen, surrounded by some very busy friends. She wasn't the only one covered with flour or the only one who hadn't realized that a rolling pin was the long, round thing with handles at each end. With her very own ears she had heard Dee say she had never known milk came in little cans. And a boy from Oakley Prep had asked, aloud, what kind of tree cinnamon grew on. A girl Jane knew for a fact was a straight-A student had neglected to pit the cherries she'd used in her pie. "It looks really good," Merrie told the distraught girl, "but I'm afraid we'd be sued for ruining some customer's dentures."

Jane sat on the stool, wrapped in a long white apron, relaxing in the warmth of the kitchen. They had been so busy since Sunday. Having the afternoons off had helped, but their days had still been packed full. Enthusiasm for what they were doing had helped, too. Knowing for a fact that their carnival was going to take place had erased most of their fatigue. They had worked long hours without complaint. The sun had stayed visible, drying out both the campus and the lumber. The dunk tank had been emptied and refilled, the booths reconstructed, both chores done with the aid of the maintenance workers. Word had reached them of the students' efforts on their behalf and they had showed their appreciation by working from dawn until dark.

Now that it was all coming together so beautifully, Jane did *not* want to go home. It wasn't fair.

So, even though she knew her parents would never be impressed by a pie, it was the only thing she could think of to do. And who knew? Maybe Andy was right. She so often was.

"Merrie," Jane called to a housemother busy explaining to a girl that you don't toss pie crust up in the air the way you do pizza crust, "I just ripped a hole in my crust big enough to drive a truck through. Got any glue?"

CHAPTER
TWENTY-FIVE

Jane knew she was the only resident of Baker House who awoke on Wednesday morning filled with dread instead of anticipation.

Cary had been so sweet the night before. After they'd finished what she called The Cook's Comedy Hour, he had walked her back to Baker. They'd stopped at the wishing well, sitting down on its stone ledge.

"This is a rotten time for you to leave," he said, taking her hand. "Now that the strike is over, we wouldn't have anything to argue about."

Jane forced a laugh. "We will *always* have something to argue about. But you're right. This is a rotten time to leave. Everyone else is so excited about the carnival. I feel like I'm on the outside, looking in. I don't like the feeling."

"You're not used to it." Cary shook his head.

"Do you think it would help if I spoke to your folks?"

Jane almost smiled. Only Cary would call the Barretts "folks." "No, but thanks." Because she was feeling so much pain at the thought of leaving, and because she didn't want Cary sensing her pain, she changed the subject. "I'll see you when school gets out. That's only a few weeks from now. I guess I can survive until then."

He had hugged her then and she'd been careful not to cry or to hug him too tightly.

But now, waking to the sound of her roommates chattering excitedly about the opening of the carnival that night, her heart felt like a chunk of cement.

"I'm not going peacefully," she announced suddenly, startling her roommates. "They'll have to drag me."

"Well, great!" Andy said with a smile. "I'm glad to hear it. And don't forget you have your pie as a bargaining tool."

They all stared at the odd lump sitting on Jane's nightstand. It looked like something that had been fashioned out of clay by a very small and perhaps near-sighted child.

"Yeah," Toby said doubtfully. "You could always threaten to make them eat some of it. That should do it."

Jane burst into laughter and her roommates followed suit. The laughter, unlike the tears Jane might have shed, left them all feeling curiously giddy and light-hearted.

"C'mon," Andy said, gasping for breath, "let's get going. We've got lots to do today."

During the storm the electricity hadn't been off long enough to ruin the supplies in the freezer, so no additional trips to town for more supplies had been necessary. During the afternoon, they popped endless batches of popcorn, loaded dry-ice-lined coolers with ice cream bars and cans of soda. They made sandwitches, tortillas and tacos (Toby's idea), and kept them warm or cold in the big warming oven and refrigerator.

At five o'clock, as many people as Andy could round up began bringing food out from the kitchen. By five-thirty-five, the Canby Hall Almost Summer Carnival was ready to open. Students were already in charge of the game booths, the food booths, and the long, low table covered with the pie-baking contest entries.

While everyone else rushed around breathlessly, Jane paced slowly back and forth on the steps of Baker House. She had no suitcases in her hands or at her feet. She had no intention of making this whole deal easy on her parents. If they wanted her luggage to go back to Boston with her, they'd just have to go upstairs and get it. Three flights of stairs just might discourage them.

They arrived at six on the dot, which didn't surprise Jane in the least. Punctuality was as important to them as proper diction. Jane sighed as the sleek gray car pulled up in front of her. Then she limped down to greet them.

"Oh, you poor darling!" her mother said, even though Jane had carefully hidden her bandaged ankles under blue pleated trousers. Ms. Barrett was her usual elegant self in a pale green silk dress and matching heeled sandals — hardly the right sort of clothes for walking around a still-damp campus, but Jane was determined to show her parents around the carnival. Like I said, she thought with firm resolve, I'm not going peacefully. *Or* quickly.

"Come, darling," her mother said, "let's go get your things. I did expect someone to bring your luggage down for you."

"Everyone's busy with the carnival," Jane said cheerfully. "Why don't we go see how things are going? I'm sure you're tired of sitting, and after coming all that way, you might as well see what we've been working so hard on. Everything has worked out just fine. And the strike is over now, so . . ."

"Yes, we know," her mother said. Her father, in a gray silk suit and cranberry tie, nodded. "Too bad it didn't happen before you had your terrible ordeal. I won't rest until you're safely at home recuperating."

"Mother, I have never had a terrible ordeal in my life. It was just a little accident and I'm fine now. The *ordeal* is having to go home just as the carnival is starting. It seems to me if you're going to drag me away from where I really want to be, you can at least take a look around first. I want to see if people are having a good time. You'll love it, I promise. Come on!"

Sensing that it was the only way to ever get Jane into the car, and cramped from the long drive, the Barretts agreed to the walk. As they headed toward the carnival booths, Jane thought how strange a trio they must make: her parents dressed more for a fine restaurant than a carnival, and she limping, next to them. Only superb control kept her from giggling.

Her promise to her parents that they would love the carnival seemed destined to go unfulfilled. Her mother's heels sank into the still-spongy ground, collecting bits of earth as they moved across campus. They passed the dunk tank just as Cary got dumped by Andy's deadly accurate pitch and water splashed across the silk suit and the silk dress, leaving little spots like measles on the fabric. As if that weren't bad enough, her mother stated proudly that she never, ever allowed popcorn anywhere near her mouth, and her father, upon expressing hunger, sniffed at Jane's suggestion that he try a submarine sandwich from a food booth.

The campus was filling up with people, all of whom seemed to be having a good time. But Jane felt as if she were moving through a bad dream. This wasn't working. Not at all. She might as well give up and go jump into the car right now.

But then they were standing in front of the

ring-toss booth and her father was taking off his jacket and handing it to her mother, who was . . . smiling? Her mother was smiling! Why? She had mud on her shoes, she hated popcorn, and there were water spots on her dress. But she was most definitely smiling.

Jane wasn't sure how it had happened. They had approached the ring-toss booth, run by a boy from Oakley Prep. There was a small crowd around it. Her father hardly seemed to notice it at first. Then, when he did, and realized what kind of game the booth contained, he had stood there looking at it for several minutes. Jane hadn't been paying that much attention until the jacket came off. Now, she couldn't believe what she was seeing.

The crowd milled around them, laughing and chattering. But above the noise, Jane heard her mother say, "Your father hasn't done this in years," as Mr. Barrett paid the boy a quarter and received three rings in exchange. His challenge was to toss the rings so they looped themselves over velvet-covered blocks of wood in different shapes and sizes. Before he started, he rolled his shirtsleeves up to his elbow.

Jane watched. He hadn't done this in years? Was that what her mother had said? Didn't that mean her father had actually played a ring-toss game somewhere, sometime, before now? Really?

"Jane, your mouth is open," Andy said,

coming up behind her. "You'll catch flies. What gives?"

And Cary, who had changed into dry clothes after his dunking, said, "Hey, Jane, look at that! Your dad's really getting into the spirit of things. That's neat!"

Yes, it *was* neat. Even though he didn't place a single ring on his first three throws. But it was still neat, because he tried again. When he missed all three the second time, Jane was sure he'd give up and turn away in disgust. But he didn't. And the third try turned out to be the lucky one. Her tall, handsome father was getting the hang of it now, and when two of the rings hit their targets, the crowd roared its approval. Mr. Barrett looked pleased. He plunked down another quarter.

"I don't believe this," Jane whispered to Toby, who had just arrived with Randy Crowell in tow. "He's actually having fun!"

Her mother overheard her and laughed. "He's going to win that panda bear for me," she said confidently, pointing to one of the stuffed animals donated by a local department store. "I guarantee it."

A panda? Her mother wanted a stuffed panda?

"He did it once before," Ms. Barrett added softly. "A long, long time ago."

Cary put an arm around Jane's shoulders. "Things are looking up," he whispered. "They're both smiling."

It was true. They were. Hope began to beat butterfly wings against Jane's chest. If she could just keep them in this strange but wonderful mood. . . .

No problem. Her father, his face flushed with triumph, traded the suit jacket his wife had been carrying for the stuffed panda he had won. Her eyes beamed as she cuddled it close to the water-spotted silk dress. She looked at her husband in a way that Jane couldn't remember ever having seen before.

Jane's ankles were beginning to throb, but she didn't utter one syllable of complaint. So, when her parents moved from the ring-toss booth to the next one, she went with them. So did most of the crowd.

During the course of the evening, her father won at various games two boxes of candy, a coupon for a free lube job at Arnie's Garage in the village, a small stuffed monkey which he presented to Jane with great dignity, and a floral centerpiece. He gave all of them but the monkey to her mother, who handed them, queenlike, to Matt and Cary to hold for her. Jane held up very well considering her parents' strange behavior, until they bought, and ate, two tacos apiece.

Then, she sank down on a bench and asked Cary in a bewildered voice, "Who *are* these people?"

"They're the people who came to take you home," Cary answered, "and unless I miss my guess, you can unpack now."

And looking at her parents, standing slightly apart from the crowd, spilling little traces of tacos on their silk garments and looking blissfully happy, Jane realized that Cary was right. She wouldn't be going home tonight. Or tomorrow. Glancing at her watch, she wondered if her parents would even be returning to Boston before tomorrow. It was late. That was a long drive. And they didn't seem ready even now to tear themselves away.

Well, she wasn't going to worry about them. There was a lovely inn just this side of the village. Her mother would love it. Not her Boston mother, who preferred luxurious hotels with doormen, but her carnival mother who ate tacos and hugged a big panda bear. She would adore the inn.

Andy and Matt, Toby and Randy joined them, paper-wrapped tacos in hand.

They all walked to the booth where the pies were displayed. "Bad news, Jane," Andy said with a gleam in her eye. "A boy named Russell Swanson won the pie-baking contest, with his Apple Crumb Pie recipe. Too bad."

Cary laughed, "Well, the judges had good taste." Jane teasingly picked up her pie and held it in one hand, poised, ready to throw at Cary. He ducked and put his arms around his head as, laughingly, Jane put her pie back on the shelf.

Jane just smiled and looked away from Cary to her parents.

Andy grinned. "I take it you'll be with us

for a while longer," she told Jane, tipping her head toward Mr. and Mrs. Barrett. "Isn't that amazing? The transformation, I mean? But then," she added glibly, "a really good carnival will do that."

Matt smiled at her. "Is this a really good carnival?"

"Are you kidding? Look at this crowd! Are they happy or are they happy?"

"Seems to me," Toby said thoughtfully, "that this Canby Hall/Oakley Prep Almost Summer Carnival is just about the best!" Privately, she was thinking it wouldn't be totally perfect until Neal arrived on Friday evening to spend the weekend. But for now, it was just plain almost perfect.

Andy sighed happily. "When you think about what we went through. . . . But it was all worth it, wasn't it?"

Jane smiled, first at her parents, who smiled back rather absent-mindedly, then at Cary, and then at her friends. "Yes," she said, "it was all definitely worth it. Now where," she asked, "is my taco?"

Does the cute new girl in Baker House have Andy, Jane, and Toby completely fooled? To find out, read The Girls of Canby Hall #23, BUT SHE'S SO CUTE!